Patriot Colonel:
The Life & Times of Francis Locke

A historical novel by
Eliott Secrest

Patriot Colonel: The Life & Times of Francis Locke is a work of historical fiction. Aside from well-documented real people, events, places, businesses, and organizations that are part of the story, all names, characters, locations, businesses, organizations, and incidents are fictional or used creatively by the author. Any similarity to actual persons, living or dead, events, or places is purely coincidental. Every effort has been made to depict specific historical facts accurately; however, some creative liberties have been taken for storytelling. Some dates are approximate or have been adjusted to fit the fictional narrative.

Published by Mill Bridge Press
Raleigh, North Carolina, USA

ISBN: 9798218849993
Printed in the United States of America.

Second Edition
Cover design by 100covers.com

CONTENTS

Preface

Patriot Colonel: The Life & Times of Francis Locke is a work of historical fiction based on a real person, Francis Locke. Locke's story is one of courage, leadership, and pivotal moments that helped shape the nation's future and secured the freedoms we enjoy today. From daring skirmishes to decisive battles against Loyalists and the British Army, Locke's impact on history is undeniable.

Born in 1722 in Northern Ireland, Francis Locke emigrated to America with his family at a young age. Throughout his life in America, he worked as a farmer, planter, trader, businessman, carpenter, tavern owner, politician, sheriff, coroner, and state attorney. However, his most notable contribution to history was serving as a decorated colonel during the American Revolutionary War. Yet, despite his many business, political, and military pursuits, Francis never lost sight of the importance of family; he was a devoted son and brother, and a loving husband and father.

Set against the backdrop of colonial America, this historical fiction novel paints a vivid picture of the struggles and triumphs of a man who was not born in America but embodied the American spirit—a spirit forged from being on the wrong side of a class system that favored noble birth over education and hard work; a spirit shaped by the political struggles between the haves and the have-nots; a spirit fueled by the fight for freedom from an oppressive monarchy; and a spirit born from the desire to worship freely, not as the government dictates. This American spirit inspired and motivated Francis Locke.

After the untimely death of his father, John Locke, Francis, as the oldest son, became the head of the family at only twenty-two. He took on the responsibility of caring for his widowed mother and six siblings, whose ages ranged from two to sixteen. At twenty-six, Francis and his family endured the dangers and hardships along the Great Wagon Road from Pennsylvania to North Carolina, where he purchased a large tract of land, married, built a house, cleared the land, and began farming. Along with his brother, he operated a fleet of wagons that transported goods between various frontier settlements and the main commercial centers of Salisbury and Salem, North Carolina, and Charles Town (now Charleston), South Carolina. He also operated a tavern and served as the county sheriff and coroner.

When called to defend his young country, Francis served in the Rowan County, North Carolina, militia as an ensign before rising to the rank of colonel, playing a crucial role in several key battles during the Southern campaign of the Revolutionary War. After the war, Francis studied law and became a lawyer, eventually rising to the position of State Attorney for Rowan County.

Francis Locke may not be as well known in history as his contemporaries, such as George Washington, Patrick Henry, Thomas Jefferson, or Francis Marion (the "Swamp Fox"). Still, he is no less of an American hero. Locke's story is an essential part of the American story because it offers a unique perspective on our nation's early years.

A note on current versus historical language, terminology, and customs: First, 18th-century English differs from modern usage. This work employs contemporary English for improved clarity. Second, every effort has been made to accurately reflect 18th-century culture, including terms like "Indians" for Native Americans and references to slavery, even if, by today's standards, these may be offensive.

Eliott Secrest
Raleigh, North Carolina

1
Off to America

In early August 1731, the Dragon, a fully rigged three-masted barque, was preparing to sail from Belfast, Northern Ireland, to Philadelphia in the British colony of Pennsylvania. It had recently arrived from Rotterdam with passengers from Europe. While docked in Belfast, more passengers from Ireland and Scotland boarded, and the crew loaded additional cargo. The ship was scheduled to depart within the hour, carrying 105 passengers and their luggage, along with a cargo of letters, cloth, furniture, tools, and tea.

John Locke hurried along the bustling dock, carrying his two-year-old son, Matthew. The sun was barely over the horizon, and seabirds soared and called overhead as he glanced back at Eliza, his wife, about 20 feet behind him.

"Eliza, please be quick! Passengers are boarding the ship!" John urged.

Eliza, four months pregnant, hurried along, holding the hands of four-year-old John Jr., whom they called Jack, and three-year-old George, thinking, *I don't understand the rush! The ship isn't ready to leave, and passengers are still boarding! The children can only walk so fast, and I can't in my condition!*

"I'm hurrying as fast as I can with the boys, John. Please wait for me!" Eliza pleaded.

John, impatient to board, stopped to wait for Eliza, the smell of salt and dead fish drifting past his nose. When she caught up with him, she noticed him glancing anxiously back down the dock while other passengers rushed past.

"Where is Francis?" Eliza asked with a worried look. "I thought he was with you!"

"He was here with me just a moment ago!" John exclaimed, his voice filled with frustration as he scanned the busy dock in the dim light of early morning, frantically searching for his oldest son.

Eliza held Matthew in her arms and waited with the other children while John returned down the dock to look for his son.

As he passed the barnacle-encrusted pilings, stacks of cargo, and dodged passengers heading toward the ship, his mind raced. *Now, where could that boy have gone? I told him to stay with me! The ship will leave soon!*

Francis, a typical nine-year-old boy, was adventurous, curious, fearless, and outgoing. He had long auburn hair pulled back and loosely tied at the back of his head, with some strands falling over his brown eyes. His cheeks and nose were dotted with freckles from days spent playing in the sun. He wore a tan shirt with puffed sleeves, black knickers, long white stockings, a waistcoat, and simple brown shoes.

John returned shortly without finding Francis. As he approached his family, he exclaimed, "I searched all the way back down the dock, and I didn't see him! Maybe he's gone ahead of us."

Eliza, also frantically searching for her son, turned and eventually spotted the boy ahead.

"There he is!" she declared, pointing at Francis, who was staring at the tall masts of the ship with wide eyes and an open mouth as he walked up the wooden gangway, surrounded by other passengers.

John noticed him at the same time and yelled, "Francis, wait for us! I told you to stay with me!"

Francis stopped walking up the gangway but kept glancing up at the tall masts, fascinated by sailors climbing the rigging and sitting on the yardarms high above the deck.

"Yes, Father," he replied.

When the family reunited, walked up the gangway, and stepped aboard, the captain greeted them eagerly. "Welcome aboard, Mr. Locke! What a nice-looking family you have! I shall have Mr. Smith, my first mate, escort you to your cabin."

John bowed. "Thank you, Captain." Then, he turned to Mr. Smith and asked, "Have our possessions been loaded aboard, sir?"

"Yes, sir, they are securely stored in the hold, and the chest with your belongings has been delivered to your cabin. Please follow me."

Mr. Smith wore a blue-and-white striped shirt and dark canvas breeches that ended at the knees. His long, light brown hair was tied back and covered with a Monmouth cap, and, like most crew members, he was barefoot to prevent slipping on wet decks and to better grip the rigging.

As the family followed Mr. Smith to their cabin at the stern, Francis's curiosity was obvious.

"How big is this ship, sir?" Francis asked.

Mr. Smith motioned, "She's 151 feet long and 30 feet wide at midship."

"Is she fast?"

"She will do about 8 knots with favorable winds."

"How many sailors are on the ship?" Francis asked as he watched several sailors preparing for the voyage.

"There are 21 crew members, including the captain."

"How long will the voyage take?" Francis asked.

"About two months, give or take a week or two, depending on the winds."

"Will we see any whales? Or sharks?"

"You probably will. There are plenty of whales and sharks in the ocean."

As the family arrived at their cabin, John groaned, "My goodness, Francis. That's enough questions!"

"Yes, sir," Francis replied.

Mr. Smith opened the door to the cabin and stepped aside to let the family enter. "Here are your quarters, Mr. Locke. I trust you will be comfortable here."

John bowed his head. "Thank you, sir. I am sure we will."

John spent his youth aboard ships owned by his father's company, transporting passengers between Europe, England,

Ireland, and the American colonies. When John reached adulthood, his father retired and handed control of the company over to him. The Dragon was a vessel in his fleet. As the owner, John enjoyed a private cabin near the captain's quarters and below the poop deck at the stern. Most passengers were in cramped berthing areas below deck.

The cabin was small, about fifteen by twelve feet, but unlike the berthing areas below decks, it provided some privacy for the family. The heavy oak door swung open onto the main deck, and the cabin deck, walls, and ceiling were all made of oak. Two small wooden beds with straw mattresses and several straw mats offered sleeping space. The rear wall at the stern had a window that could be opened for ventilation, but since it was closed, the cabin smelled of old wood and damp straw. The family's provisions, including clothing and food, were stored in the sea chest, which had been delivered to the room by crew members. Their other belongings—furniture, cooking utensils, tools, a musket, and a pistol—needed in America, were kept in the hold along with the rest of the cargo.

John and his wife, Mary Elizabeth, whom he affectionately called Eliza, hailed from Northern Ireland. They had planned and saved for their move to the American colonies for several years.

John, 31, was tall, with broad shoulders and a muscular build, having spent many years at sea. His eyes sparkled blue like the ocean, and his light brown hair was long and tied back. He wore a white shirt with puffed sleeves and a brown waistcoat, paired with black trousers that reached his knees and white stockings. Black shoes with brass buckles and a black tricorne hat completed his outfit.

Eliza, 27, stood five feet two inches tall, with delicate features, green eyes, and dark red hair that flowed to the middle of her back. Her skin was lightly sprinkled with freckles on her small, perfectly shaped cheeks and nose. As she was expecting, she showed a bump on her belly. She wore a simple, long, floral-patterned dress, stockings, plain leather shoes with low heels, and a ruffled bonnet.

John first saw Eliza one spring evening in 1718, as she stood next to an older man, presumably her father, across the room at a ball hosted at the Hyde family estate near Belfast. Her natural beauty, with emerald eyes and a petite stature, captivated him; his heart skipped a beat when their eyes met, and she smiled at him. As he approached her to ask her to dance, she initially declined, blushing and fanning herself. However, with John's persistent encouragement and a nod from her father, she eventually agreed, extending her hand to him. He guided her onto the dance floor, where they danced to the music of cellos and violins. As the dance ended, he returned her to her father. Since social decorum only allowed a gentleman to dance a maximum of two dances with a young lady during the evening, John waited and asked her for the last dance of the night.

When the last dance ended, John took Eliza back to her father and asked for permission to visit her the following week, which her father granted. Over the next year, John and Eliza attended social events, balls, and theater outings together, closely supervised by her father.

One evening, John visited Eliza's house dressed in formal attire and holding a bouquet of red roses. The butler greeted him at the door and led him to Eliza's father in the library.

"Welcome, Mr. Locke. How may I be of service?" Eliza's father asked.

John, with sweat on his brow, began, "Sir, I have developed a deep admiration for Eliza over the past year. I have come tonight to ask for her hand in marriage, and I respectfully seek your blessing."

Knowing this moment would eventually arrive, Eliza's father looked directly into John's eyes. "Mr. Locke, I have developed a genuine respect for you as a gentleman. I have observed the way you treat my daughter, as well as the glow in her eyes when she's in your company."

He paused for what felt like an eternity to John before finally saying, "I would be honored to have you as a son-in-law; therefore, you have my blessing."

John, grinning, could barely hold back his happiness. "Thank you, sir!"

Eliza's father continued, "Eliza is in the parlor. You have my blessing, but you do not have Eliza's answer. I suggest you ask her yourself!"

"Thank you, sir. I will!" John replied, bowed, and headed to the parlor.

As John entered, Eliza was sitting on a settee reading a book. She looked up, and when their eyes met, she put the book down and smiled, her eyes shining at the sight of him. Holding the bouquet of roses, he knelt, gently took her hand, kissed it, and looked into her eyes.

"Eliza, we have become close over the past year. I miss your touch when we're apart, and I think of you constantly. I can't live without you, so with your father's gracious approval and blessing, I humbly ask: Will you do me the great honor of becoming my wife? I will love and cherish you forever with all my heart."

He kissed her hand again and continued gazing into her eyes. Blushing and with tears of joy in her eyes, Eliza immediately consented to his proposal. In 1719, they married in Belfast and began their life together. Three years later, they were blessed with a son whom they named Francis.

◆◆◆

Under a clear blue sky, with an outgoing tide and steady wind, the Dragon set sail at 7:51 AM on August 3, 1731. The sun was shining brightly, its rays warming the lingering chill in the early morning air.

"Mr. Smith, cast off all lines and prepare to make way," the captain ordered the first mate, Mr. Smith, from the poop deck.

"Aye, Captain," Mr. Smith replied from the main deck.

Mr. Smith turned to Mr. McDougal, the bosun, beside the mainmast. "Mr. McDougal, prepare to make way. Cast off all lines and unfurl the bowsprit sails. Hoist the flag."

The flag, known as the Green Ensign, identified Irish merchant marine ships and featured a green field with a gold Irish harp and the Union Jack in the upper left corner.

"Aye, sir," Mr. McDougal answered, then instructed the sailors on the main deck. "Cast off the bow and stern lines. Unfurl and secure the sails on the bowsprit. Hoist the flag. Fasten all hatches."

As the sailors in the crew carried out the bosun's orders, the unfurled bowsprit sails caught the wind, and the helmsman steered the ship away from the dock, firmly gripping the wheel at the helm.

As the ship rounded Copeland Island and entered the Irish Sea, the captain called out, "Mr. Smith, set sail," and to the sailor at the helm, "Set a course for south by southeast."

With this order, the sailors in the riggings of the mizzenmast unfurled its sails, while other sailors, high on the mainmasts and foremast, released the square-rigged sails from the yardarms. The sails cracked sharply as they filled with wind, propelling the ship swiftly through the three-foot waves as seabirds squawked and circled the vessel, hoping for a meal.

◆ ◆ ◆

By noon, excitement and anticipation soared as the ship rounded the southern coast of Ireland and entered the North Atlantic Ocean. A steady easterly breeze blew, and the sky was clear. Sunlight sparkled on the water, and the invigorating scent of the sea permeated the air as the ship smoothly cut through the moderate, five-foot swells. It was a glorious day to be at sea.

The passengers were eager to begin their journey to a new home in the American colonies, and the Locke family was no exception. After they had settled into their cabin, John and Eliza took the children out onto the main deck to enjoy the fresh air and sights. Eliza stood under the mainmast and held Jack and George by their hands. John held Matthew and stood beside Francis as they leaned over the railing amidships, looking down at the water.

With fear in her eyes, Eliza shouted, "John, please stay away from the railing with the baby in your arms!"

Don't worry, Eliza. I've got him. We're watching the porpoises race the ship.

"Look, Mother! Porpoises!" Francis yelled.

George and Jack, held tightly by Eliza, desperately tried to wiggle free so they could see the porpoises too.

Eliza, a bit annoyed, rolled her eyes, shook her head, and headed toward the stern. "John, please bring Matthew to our cabin. It's time for his feeding, and the other boys are hungry."

"I'm starving!" Francis declared as he raced ahead of his father toward the cabin.

Back in their cabin, Eliza cared for Matthew while John passed out dried fruit and nuts to the other children.

Because of the ship's constant movement, walking and moving around were difficult. The children, however, didn't mind. They played a game where they tried to stand without falling or holding onto anything. As the oldest, Francis always won because his younger siblings would giggle and deliberately fall on their bottoms.

After he helped Eliza care for the younger children and get them settled for their afternoon naps, John asked Francis, "Would you like to go with me to the poop deck to discuss the voyage with the captain?"

Francis quickly jumped up from the straw mattress he was sitting on. "I would love to, Father!"

John and Francis climbed the stairs and approached the captain, who stood beside a crew member at the helm, watching the sails.

Captain Charles Hargrave, of medium build and muscular, had long, dark hair now graying at the temples and piercing black eyes. He wore a white linen shirt under a brown vest and loose-fitting, dark green breeches that reached his knees. His black coat had large lapels and cuffs adorned with brass buttons. Stockings, black leather shoes, and a black tricorne hat completed the outfit.

Originally from Londonderry, he came from a family with a rich history of seafarers. At twelve, he joined the Irish merchant marine as a cabin boy and ship's apprentice. After seven years of apprenticeship, he moved up through the ranks and eventually became the captain of the Dragon after 28 years at sea.

"Good afternoon, Captain!" John said as he bowed his head.

"Good afternoon, Mr. Locke. How are you and your family faring? Are your accommodations suitable?"

"We are well, and the cabin suits us just fine, thank you. It's definitely a beautiful, sunny day, and the winds are strong!"

"Yes, the wind is filling the sails, and we are making good headway!"

John placed a hand on Francis's shoulder. "Captain, allow me to present my oldest son, Francis. Francis, this is Captain Hargrave, one of my most experienced captains."

Francis looked up at the captain with admiration. "I am pleased to meet you, sir."

"The delight is mine. I trust you will have an enjoyable voyage."

"Yes, sir," Francis replied. Then, he pointed at the big wheel. "Is that how you steer the ship?"

"Yes, that is called the helm; the sailor behind it is the helmsman. Would you like to steer the ship?"

"Yes, sir, I would!" exclaimed Francis as he grabbed the wheel.

Although the helmsman was assisting, Francis grinned from ear to ear and was delighted in thinking he was steering the ship.

John turned to the captain and said, "Captain, I want you to know that I have sold the company, effective January 1st."

The captain looked at John with fear in his eyes. "Oh? I hope I can continue as captain of the Dragon with the new owner!"

"The new owner isn't planning to make any changes, so there's nothing to worry about. I also told him you're my most experienced captain."

"Thank you," the captain replied with a relieved expression. "Why are you selling the company?"

"Managing a company of this size from the colonies would be difficult."

"I completely understand. It has been a pleasure to sail the Dragon under your leadership, and I wish you the very best."

"Thank you, sir," John replied.

Then, John looked at the horizon and said, "This is the time of year for storms in the Atlantic. I hope we do not encounter any."

"There is always that chance. As you know, between June and November, hurricanes of considerable severity may occur; however, God willing, we will reach Philadelphia with minimal trouble. I plan to arrive in that fair city by late September or early October."

The wind had shifted slightly, so the captain leaned over the railing of the poop deck and barked an order to the first mate on the main deck below: "Mr. Smith, tend to the sails on the bowsprit."

"Aye, captain," Mr. Smith replied, then shouted to the bosun, "Mr. Barrow, trim the foresail on the bowsprit. Keep a sharp eye out now!"

Seeing that the captain was occupied, John headed toward the stairs that led down to the main deck. "Captain, we will take our leave and let you attend to your duties. Good day, sir. Come along, Francis."

"Good day to you as well, Mr. Locke, and also to you, Master Francis," the captain replied as he turned his attention to the helm.

When John and Francis reentered their cabin, the older children were napping, and from the smell, he knew Eliza had changed Matthew's nappy. John immediately opened the window to get rid of the smell.

"John, the children are resting. Can you please stay here with them while I go clean this soiled nappy?" Eliza asked.

"Alright."

Eliza laid Matthew on the bed, picked up the soiled nappy, and headed for the door. On the main deck, she grabbed the wash bucket tied to the railing with a rope and lowered it into the sea. After she pulled the bucket of saltwater back up, she washed the soiled nappy in it, wrung it out, and hung it on a line stretching from the mainmast to the mizzenmast to dry. She then emptied the bucket of soiled saltwater back into the sea. This chore would be repeated multiple times daily for the rest of the voyage.

Before she returned to the cabin, Eliza, enjoying the sun and fresh air, strolled along the main deck toward the bow. As she looked out at the sea, her thoughts wandered to simpler, easier times in Belfast. *I wonder whether we made the right decision in coming to America? I detest the cramped conditions on this ship, and I worry about the children's safety and well-being here. Life was so good in Belfast! My days were spent lounging, reading, or socializing with my friends. Oh, how I already miss them!*

As she passed the mainmast and approached the galley, she noticed a woman standing by the railing, watching the bow of the ship slice through the waves.

"Good afternoon," Eliza said as she approached the woman.

"Good afternoon to you. It is a beautiful day!" answered the woman.

"It certainly is, and the sun feels nice," Eliza replied as she stepped up to the railing beside the woman. "I am Eliza Locke. Whom do I have the pleasure of addressing?"

"My name is Hannah Murphy."

Hannah was short and stout, with long, dark brown hair that shone in the afternoon sun. She wore a simple cotton dress that reached her calves, plain brown leather shoes, and a flowered bonnet. She smiled warmly, and her brown eyes sparkled as she introduced herself.

"It is a pleasure to make your acquaintance, Hannah. Where are you from?" Eliz asked.

"I am from Kilrea in Northern Ireland."

"I am from Northern Ireland as well! My husband and I are from Belfast."

"It is a small world! My husband is a farmer, and Belfast is where we used to sell our produce," Hannah replied.

"My cook might have bought some of your produce! Where is your husband?"

"My husband, Ian, is with the children below decks."

"How many children do you have?"

"We are blessed with two children: Connor, nine, and Aidan, seven." Hannah replied, then asked, "Do you have any children?"

Eliza leaned against the railing, her hand resting on her belly. "Yes. We have been blessed with four sons: Francis, nine; Jack, four; George, three; and Matthew, two. And as you can see, I am expecting another child."

"Wonderful! When are you due?"

"Early next year, God willing."

"We both have nine-year-old boys. I am sure they will find each other and enjoy exploring the ship together," Hannah said.

"No doubt!" Eliza replied with a knowing smile. "Why are you going to the colonies?"

"We have been scraping by on land owned by a very mean landlord," Hannah replied. "Ian wants a better life for the children and me, so we decided several years ago to start fresh in the colonies, where we can farm our own land."

"Excellent!" Eliza answered. "I wish you the very best."

The two women became so engrossed in their conversation, as they shared their backgrounds and family details, that they didn't notice the gathering clouds until it started to rain. All the passengers on the main deck hurried to their berthing areas.

"It has been very nice meeting you, Hannah. I'm sure we will see each other again. It's a long voyage!" Eliza shouted as she hurried to her cabin.

"It has been very nice meeting you, too, Eliza, and I look forward to getting to know the rest of your family," Hannah replied from the stairwell that led to the berthing areas below.

Eliza entered the cabin and sat on the bed next to John. "I just met a lady from Kilrea named Hannah Murphy. She seemed very nice. I didn't meet her husband because he was below decks with their children."

"It would be nice to have a couple to talk to during the voyage. What's her husband's name?" John asked.

"His name is Ian. He's a farmer, and they hope to buy and farm their own land in the colonies. Oh, and they have a son the same age as Francis!"

"Oh, good. I'm sure Francis would like a friend his age to spend time with during the voyage."

"Yes, that would be nice. By the way, I came in because it's raining," Eliza said.

"Yes, I can hear it hitting the window glass. We need the rain. It has been extremely hot."

"Yes, it has. Since it's raining, we might as well get some rest while the children are asleep," Eliza whispered, lying on the bed beside the children.

"That sounds wonderful. I'm tired."

As the children slept, John and Eliza lay down with them to rest and listened to the soothing sounds of the wind and rain outside.

2
The Long Voyage

A long voyage aboard a sailing ship on a vast ocean was not for the faint of heart. The berthing areas below decks were crowded, dark, and damp, with barely any ventilation, and quickly became filled with the smell of vomit, urine, soiled nappies, and unwashed bodies. Food from the galley was limited to porridge, beans, dried pork, dried biscuits, beer, and water. Most passengers also brought their own food, such as dried and fresh fruits, jerky, nuts, and raw vegetables.

After nearly three weeks of smooth sailing, calm seas, and steady winds, John and Eliza had settled into a routine of waking early, feeding and caring for the children, and spending time on deck with other passengers, enjoying the fresh air and sea breezes. The days were sultry, with little to no rain. When the sun was high in the sky, most passengers retreated to the few shaded areas on the ship, their cabins, or below deck.

After they put the children to bed at night, John and Eliza enjoyed strolling on the main deck, savoring the cool evening air and gazing at the bright moon and stars.

"Oh, look, John!" Eliza exclaimed. "The sky is beautiful tonight, and there are so many stars! There goes a shooting star! And another one!"

John leaned his back against the railing and held Eliza in his arms as the ship gently rocked with the swell of the sea. "Uh-huh. It is beautiful, and the moon is so bright!"

Eliza leaned her back against John's broad chest and savored the warmth of his body as he held her close. "John, I am excited about starting our new life in America, but I really miss the life we had in Belfast. I wonder whether we have made the right decision. I just want the children to be safe and happy."

John had visited Philadelphia during his seafaring days many years ago. "I miss Belfast and the life we had there, too. But I think you will like Philadelphia. It is very nice and will be a great place to put down some roots and raise our children."

"I sure hope so," Eliza said, trying to stay positive.

John rested his hands on Eliza's belly. "I can feel the baby moving!"

"Yes, it has been kicking me for a few days now. I hope it's a girl!"

John held Eliza close. He felt blessed to have her as his wife and the four sons she had given him.

"A daughter would be nice," he replied, kissing her neck.

Eliza placed her hands on John's, smiled, and paused for a moment. "Yes. I would like to have a little girl, but as long as all goes well, that's all that matters."

"All the same, with four boys already, we need a little girl to even things out!"

John and Eliza had become good friends with Ian and Hannah Murphy, who, along with other passengers, strolled on the deck beneath the moon and stars, enjoying the cool night air.

"Good evening, Hannah. How are you tonight?" Eliza asked as Hannah and Ian approached them.

Hannah leaned against the railing next to John and Eliza as the ship creaked from the movement of the waves. "We are well. It's such a beautiful night! How are you, John, and the children doing?"

"We're all doing well, thank you. Yes, it's a beautiful night out. There are so many stars, and I can see the Milky Way!"

John bowed his head toward Ian. "Good evening, Ian. I hope you are well."

Ian had dark brown hair tied back, covered with a tricorne hat. He was tall and lean, with tanned, muscular arms from spending hours in the sun as a farmer.

Ian leaned against the railing beside John. "Good evening, sir. I trust you and Eliza are well."

"Yes, we are well. So far, the voyage has been uneventful. God willing, we will arrive in Philadelphia safely. There is always the possibility of hurricanes at this time of year. My company lost the schooner Diligence two years ago on its way to Boston with 95 passengers and crew aboard. Most likely, they encountered a severe storm and sank. There has been no trace of the ship or anyone on board."

Ian's expression changed from pleasant to concerned. "How terrible! We must continue to pray for a safe voyage and that we will encounter no severe storms."

"Don't worry. The chance of a severe storm is low. The Dragon is strong and seaworthy, and the captain and crew are very experienced. But prayers are always comforting."

"I won't worry, but I will pray for a safe voyage!" Ian replied.

Francis and Connor Murphy, being the same age and both quite adventurous, became best friends and spent their days exploring the ship from bow to stern. They also formed friendships with several sailors who fascinated them with tales of their voyages and taught the boys how to tie some knots used on the ship.

One sailor who especially befriended the boys was James, known by his shipmates as 'Spider' for his agility while climbing the rigging.

"Here is a good knot to know," said Spider, as he showed the boys how to tie a bowline and explained its use.

While the boys practiced tying knots, Spider told them stories of his life at sea. "When I was a little older than you two, I shipped out on the Catherine. I was only twelve, and I was a cabin boy. I spent my days swabbing the deck, emptying the garbage from the galley, and cleaning out the captain's chamber pot. And man, did it stink!"

"Ugh!" Francis and Ian said together.

James continued, "One day, there was a terrible storm, and the twenty-foot waves almost swamped us! Water was surging over the bow and flowing onto the main deck like a river. The ship was lurching and heaving so much that everyone on board was throwing up. I thought we were all going to die! But eventually, the storm passed, and we pulled through. You boys should pray that we do not encounter any storms like that on this voyage!"

The boys' eyes grew wider and wider as James told his tales, while they practiced tying knots.

When the boys grew tired of exploring, listening to Spider's tales, or practicing knot-tying, they spent time near the bow, watching for whales and porpoises.

One afternoon, they spotted a pod of whales breaching the water a few hundred yards from the ship.

"There's one!" Francis exclaimed as he pointed out a whale.

"And another! Wow! That's a big one!" Connor replied, his eyes wide with excitement.

A school of porpoises raced beside the ship, about twenty yards away. The boys were fascinated as they watched the porpoises surface for air and then dive back down. The water was so clear that they saw the porpoises swimming beneath the surface. Some even jumped out of the water.

"They are so fast!" Francis exclaimed.

"Yes, and there are so many of them. How do they avoid running into each other?"

"They must be smart," Francis replied.

As the boys watched the porpoises, the lookout in the crow's nest at the top of the mainmast shouted, "Sails off the port bow!"

The two boys immediately scanned the horizon.

"I don't see a ship," Connor said.

Also on deck, John heard the lookout and Connor's comment, then approached the boys and leaned against the railing beside them.

"You can't see the ship yet. The crow's nest is very high, so the lookout can see further over the horizon than we can from the deck," John observed as he scanned the horizon.

Eventually, the boys spotted sails on the horizon, accompanied by the report of a cannon.

"There it is!" Francis shouted, pointing toward the sails.

"I see it!" Connor replied excitedly.

"They are shooting a cannon! Maybe it's pirates!"

"Are we in danger?" Francis asked his father.

"I wouldn't worry. More than likely, that's a British man-of-war," John replied. "They fired their cannon to get our attention."

As the ship approached, Francis said, "I can see a British flag on the stern!"

"And they are raising little flags!" Connor replied.

"They are sending us a message," John said, straining to see which flags had been hoisted. "They say: 'Greetings from His Majesty, King George II. Have a safe voyage.'"

As the ship came closer, Francis exclaimed, "I can see the sailors all dressed in blue and white!"

"And lots of cannons!" Connor said as they watched the ship pass.

"All this excitement is making me hungry. I'm going back to my cabin to get something to eat. Want to meet back here around dusk?" Francis asked.

"That sounds great. See you then!" Connor replied as the two friends raced toward the stern.

On the morning of September 6, shortly after the quartermaster rang four bells, the watchman woke the captain to report that the winds had died down, leaving the ship becalmed. The captain got up, dressed, and climbed the stairs to the poop deck.

At dawn, as John lay awake in bed listening to the soft breathing of Eliza and the children, he sensed that something was wrong. The ship was perfectly still; the usual rhythmic movement was missing, and even though the window was open, the air in the cabin felt stuffy. He got up, quietly dressed, and stepped out of the cabin onto the main deck. In the dim light, he saw that all the sails were slack because there was no breeze. The sunrise reflected off the smooth, glassy water as if it were a mirror, and the usual creaks and groans of the wooden hull were absent, replaced by an unsettling silence. Even the salty smell of the sea was muted.

He climbed the stairs to the poop deck and approached the captain, who was standing next to the sailor at the helm.

"Good morning, Captain. It seems the wind has died."

"Good morning. Yes, I was awakened early this morning by the night watch. As you know, this will not be a problem if it doesn't last too long. We were becalmed on my last voyage to Charles Town for nearly two weeks. We were on the verge of running out of fresh water, and our food supplies were dwindling. If the wind doesn't return by the end of the day tomorrow, I will have to ration drinking water as a precaution."

"Well, we can only pray that this calm does not last long. I will leave you to your duties. Good day to you, sir," John said as he descended the stairway to the main deck.

As John reentered his cabin, baby Matthew was crying to be fed, and Eliza was stirring.

Eliza picked up Matthew and started feeding him.

"John," she asked, "why is the ship not moving this morning?"

John sat on the sea chest beside Eliza, sweat running down his forehead. "There is no wind. This isn't unusual, and we should be fine as long as it doesn't take too long for the wind to start again. The captain said he might have to ration water."

During the days when the ship was at a standstill, the sun beat down mercilessly, and there was no comfort anywhere because of the lack of a breeze to cool things off. The sea was as smooth as glass, with barely a ripple to be seen, and the sails drooped as if exhausted from the heat. The setting sun provided some relief, but even the nights were nearly unbearable. Many passengers and crew members slept on the main deck at night because the stagnant air below deck made the conditions stuffy and almost nauseating. The captain ordered that water be rationed to one cup per person each day.

"John, this is almost intolerable. I do not know how much more the children can take. They are all burning up. Matthew's face is red, and he's not as playful as he usually is," Eliza said, with sweat on her brow and cheeks.

"Francis, go fetch a bucket of seawater," John said.

When Francis returned with the full bucket, John soaked some rags and gave them to Eliza. "Place these wet rags on the children's foreheads and around their necks to cool them."

The wet rags' cooling effect soon had the desired effect: the children cooled down, temporarily relieving their discomfort.

Five days after the winds died down, they picked up again. The sails snapped sharply as they filled with air, causing the ship to lurch forward. Crew members and passengers on deck cheered loudly, and the captain offered a prayer of thanks.

On the poop deck, the captain, who had taken a reading with his sextant, turned to the sailor at the helm. "The current has caused us to drift off course to the south. Set a northwesterly course to get back on track."

"Aye, captain," the helmsman said as he turned the wheel to put the ship on the requested course.

In the summer of 1731, the Sahara Desert in northern Africa was going through an unusually hot and dry period. As the hot easterly winds blowing across the desert met the cooler air over the seas along Africa's west coast, thunderstorms formed, and a circular pattern took shape.

By early September, the system had reached the middle of the Atlantic Ocean, generating winds of 80 miles per hour and 20-foot seas. This was a hurricane, and it was heading directly toward the British colony of North Carolina. By September 20th, the hurricane had strengthened, made landfall near Wilmington on the North Carolina coast, and was tracking northward along the Virginia coastline.

That morning, John woke at dawn and noticed that the ship was heaving more than usual and leaning significantly. He dressed quietly to avoid waking Eliza and the children, then stepped out of the cabin onto the main deck. Dark, threatening clouds gathered on the horizon, with lightning flashing across the sky and thunder rumbling in the distance. The wind had increased markedly, creating whitecaps on the sea, with waves reaching about 12 feet. The ship was tilted approximately 20 degrees because of the wind pressing against the sails. Desperately holding onto the stair railing and looking up to the poop deck, he saw the captain staring toward the southwest.

John shouted over the noise of the sails whistling in the wind, "It looks like we are in for bad weather, Captain!"

"Yes, Mr. Locke. I had hoped we could avoid this storm, but it is getting closer, and the wind has picked up considerably in the past hour. I urge you to return to your cabin for your safety and to get your family ready for the rough seas ahead."

As John headed back to his cabin, the captain shouted to the first mate on the main deck below, "Mr. Smith, storm sails."

"Aye, Captain." The helmsman replied.

"Aye, Captain," replied Mr. Smith, then, yelling to the bosun above the whistling of the wind, "Mr. McDougal, storm sails, and man the bilge pumps!"

"Aye, sir."

Upon receiving their orders, several sailors quickly and skillfully climbed the rigging of the mainmast and foremast. Holding tightly against the strong wind, they rolled up the sails and secured them to the yardarms. Other sailors scaled the rigging of the mizzenmast and bowsprit, reefing the sails as they went. Several crew members secured everything on the decks, including barrels, loose ropes, storage chests, and open hatches, while a few went below to operate the bilge pumps.

With the mainmast and foremast sails furled, and the sails on the mizzenmast and bowsprit reefed, the ship slowed considerably. As the helmsman skillfully steered the vessel to sail roughly sixty degrees into the wind and waves, the rigging began to whistle and sing as rain poured down in sheets.

Waves now reached about 15 feet in height. The ship would climb a wave, crest, and then crash into the trough between that wave and the next. As the bow plunged into the next wave, seawater would flood over the bow and sweep across the main deck, sometimes reaching depths of two to three feet. With each new wave, seawater flooded the main deck. Anything not secured, or anyone not tied down or holding on tightly, would be washed overboard.

Fortunately, no one was on the main deck. The helmsman and several sailors monitored the sails from the poop deck, which was above the water spilling over the main deck. They were hanging on for dear life even though they had tied themselves to the helm and railings with ropes as the ship lurched up and down.

John, Eliza, and the children huddled inside their cabin, praying fervently and trying their best to hold on against the ship's movement. Seawater flowed under the cabin door, covering the deck by several inches. John had already closed the window and moved the straw mats off the deck so they wouldn't get soaked. The children cried in fear while Eliza tried to comfort and reassure them.

"John, I am fearful for our lives," Eliza cried. "We should never have attempted this journey!"

John slid beside Eliza and wrapped his arms around her. "Eliza, God willing, we will get through this. This is a sturdy ship, and the captain and crew are experienced at handling it in storms. We need to stay calm to comfort the children."

Francis leaned in and asked, "Father, are we going to die?"

"No, Francis. We're going to be fine. I've faced worse storms at sea. This is frightening, but we have to stay brave for your mother and brothers."

"Yes, Father," Francis replied, clinging to the bed frame to keep from being thrown around.

Below decks, the other passengers in their dark berthing areas were being tossed about by the ship's movement, uncertain whether they would survive or perish. Seawater sloshed beneath their feet. In the darkness, Ian and Hannah held their children as they cried in fear. Nearby, other passengers cried out in panic and tried to comfort their children.

"Ian, I am so afraid this storm will sink the ship! We are all going to perish!" Hannah exclaimed.

"I know. I'm afraid too. We must pray we will survive this," Ian replied.

"The cramped conditions down here, the terrible odors, and this constant tossing up and down are making me sick!" Hannah said as she clutched her stomach.

Connor fell out of his bed from a sudden jolt of the ship. "Father, are we going to die?" he asked as he climbed back onto the bed.

"We must have faith that the captain can guide the ship through this storm," Ian said, although he was thinking to himself, *I know this is bad. I must not think about what John told me about the schooner Diligence. And I certainly cannot tell Hannah and the boys!*

The storm kept the ship pounding on the waves all day and through the night, while the passengers, frightened for their lives, tried to soothe their crying children. During the night, the top of the mainmast broke off at the yardarm and crashed down onto the main deck because of the ship's erratic movements in the waves.

Finally, on the morning of September 21, the storm subsided; the wind slowed to a moderate gale; the seas calmed considerably; and the sun occasionally peeked through the breaking clouds. By early afternoon, the wind had become moderate, and the seas were calm. Most passengers ventured onto the soaked deck, relieved to leave the confines of their berths. The crew had secured the top of the mainmast, which had fallen onto the deck, planning to replace it when the ship reached port.

The captain called out from the poop deck, "Set sail, Mr. Smith," and to the helmsman, "Set a course for southwest."

"Aye, captain."

When the crew received the orders, several sailors trimmed the mizzenmast and foremast sails, and others ascended the riggings of the mainmast and foremast, releasing the square-rigged sails from the yardarms. The sails snapped loudly as they caught the wind, and the ship quickly gained speed.

◆◆◆

Around noon on September 30, the lookout high in the crow's nest shouted out loudly, "Land ho!"

With that exclamation, passengers hurried up on deck, their eyes fixed on the east, excited that the voyage was about to end. On the eastern horizon, a sliver of sand and green appeared. Seabirds circled, calling out and searching for handouts.

More details emerged as the ship drew closer to the shore. Small sailboats could be seen just offshore, and people were walking along the beach as waves rolled onto the sand.

"Oh, John!" Eliza exclaimed, leaning over the rail to get a better look. "I'm so glad the voyage is nearly over! I can't wait to get back on dry land!"

"Me neither. The coastline is such a welcome sight!"

As the ship entered the Delaware River for the 20-mile trip upriver to Philadelphia, the crew was busy adjusting the sails, taking depth soundings from the bow, and relaying the results to the captain and helmsman at the wheel. Although the captain had traveled this river many times, storms and tides could unexpectedly shift shoals and bars, so this part of the journey required careful navigation.

The ship moved upriver at about four knots. With a prevailing wind blowing from the southeast, it would only take a few hours for the ship to reach the dock in Philadelphia.

John climbed the stairs to the poop deck for a better view as the ship passed mile after mile of woodlands, interspersed with occasional buildings and homesteads. Captain Hargrave was on the poop deck, shouting orders to the crew while overseeing the sails and direction of the ship. Most passengers were on the main deck, enjoying the sights along the river.

The captain announced loudly, "To all passengers: Welcome to the colony of Pennsylvania. We will arrive at the port of Philadelphia shortly. Please collect your belongings and prepare to disembark when we have docked. Your possessions stored in the hold will be unloaded as quickly as possible."

"Captain, it's been fifteen years since I've been in Philadelphia, so I'm sure it has changed a lot. Could you recommend suitable temporary lodging for my family upon our arrival?" John asked.

"Indeed. Philadelphia is a bustling city now. The population is about 12,000, and it continues to grow," the captain replied. "I highly recommend the Blue Anchor Tavern on Front Street. The proprietor, Mr. Jonathan Townsend, is a friend of mine, and it's an establishment I usually visit when I am in port. When you arrive there, please ask for Mr. Townsend and mention that I have recommended you to him. I am confident that you and your family will be treated with the utmost courtesy."

"Thank you for that recommendation, sir. Shall I see you there once you've finished your duties here on the ship?"

"You are welcome, and yes, I would be most honored to raise a tankard of ale with you to celebrate a successful voyage!"

"I would like that very much. I look forward to seeing you at the Blue Anchor," John said, as he turned and descended the steps to the main deck toward Eliza and the children.

As the ship rounded a bend in the river, the late afternoon sun illuminated some of the city's buildings as they came into view, and the smell of wood fires and cooked food filled the air. John was excited to see Philadelphia after being at sea for nearly two months and felt grateful for their safe arrival. His hope for the promise of America and its opportunities was about to be fulfilled.

3
Philadelphia

Once the Dragon's crew secured the ship to the dock and set up the gangway, the passengers, thankful to have arrived safely, disembarked. As John, Eliza, and the children stood on the busy wharf, which was crowded with people, the crew unloaded the cargo. Many people greeted and hugged friends and family members who had just gotten off the ship.

Holding Matthew in her arms, Eliza stood on the dock with the other boys gathered around and said, "Oh, John, it feels so good to be back on dry land, but I still feel like I'm swaying!"

"It certainly does. It has been a long, arduous journey, and I thank God that we made it safely."

John scanned the bustling dock for transport of their belongings after the cargo was unloaded, and he confirmed that everything of theirs was accounted for.

John said to Eliza, "Stay here with the children; I'll find someone to help us carry our things."

Seeing a man with a two-wheeled, horse-drawn cart, he approached and asked, "Good sir, I have just arrived in this fine city on the ship Dragon. We have several large chests, some furniture, and a box of tools that have been unloaded. Are you available for hire to transport those items for me?"

Yes, sir, I am available for hire. I can load and transport your possessions anywhere in the city you need.

"We hope to get a room at the Blue Anchor Tavern. Are you familiar with that establishment?"

"I am very familiar with the Blue Anchor. It's just a short walk down Front Street, which you can see right over there," the man said, pointing to the street beside the dock.

"Thank you, sir," John said. Then, as he pointed to where Eliza and the children stood beside their belongings, he added, "Over there, where my family is standing, are the items that need to be loaded. What would you charge for transporting those items to the Blue Anchor Tavern?"

The man looked at the items, mentally calculating how many could be loaded and transported.

"That will be four pounds, sir."

"You may consider yourself hired. Please take them to the Blue Anchor Tavern. I will meet you there and pay you when you arrive."

"Look, John! There's a dress shop and a furniture store over there," Eliza said, pointing at the shops as they walked down Front Street.

John held Matthew as he paused to look in the window of a hardware store. "Philadelphia has grown since I was last here! It is definitely bigger than Belfast."

Francis, eager to see the sights of this new city, hurried ahead of the rest of the family and paused in front of a confectionery shop with a window display of molasses candy, sugarplums, and nut brittle.

As the family caught up with Francis, he asked, "Oh, Mother! Can we have some candy?"

Eliza desperately tried to pull Jack and George away from the window. "We need to go to the tavern and find a room first. Plus, it's past time for supper. Maybe tomorrow."

"Yes, Mother," Francis responded, a bit disappointed. "How far is the tavern? I'm starving!"

"Just down the street," John replied.

After a brief walk, John, Eliza, and the children reached the Blue Anchor Tavern, a two-story clapboard building painted blue with porches on the front of both levels. The sign displayed on the building advertised the tavern, which featured a large blue anchor, and offered rooms and meals. The tavern overlooked the river and the docks along Front Street.

John and Francis walked up the steps to the tavern's front door and entered while Eliza and the other children rested on a bench beneath an oak tree outside. Inside, a stairwell led to the second floor. To the right was a small dining room with tables and chairs covered in red-and-white gingham tablecloths, complemented by a large fireplace on the side wall. To the left was a spacious room with tables and chairs, an enormous stone fireplace topped with a rough-hewn oak mantel, and a long bar against the back wall.

John approached a man standing by the stairs. "Good day, sir. Could you please tell me where I can find Mr. Jonathan Townsend?"

The man was short and stocky, with a full gray beard and brown eyes. His long, graying hair was tied back behind his head. He wore a light-blue, long-sleeved shirt with a short collar, knee-length breeches, a waistcoat, and white stockings covering his lower legs. His brown leather shoes with brass buckles showed signs of heavy wear.

"I am Jonathan Townsend. To whom do I have the pleasure of speaking?"

John bowed his head. "My name is John Locke. I arrived today on a ship from Northern Ireland, and this is my oldest son, Francis."

Mr. Townsend nodded to John and Francis. "It is wonderful to meet you, Mr. Locke, and you, Master Francis. Welcome to our fair city. How can I assist you?"

"Captain Charles Hargrave, our vessel's captain, kindly recommended your establishment so my family and I can find suitable lodging until I secure a permanent residence. My wife and three of my children are waiting outside."

"Ah, Captain Hargrave is a good friend of mine. He always visits the Blue Anchor whenever the Dragon is in port. I trust you had a successful voyage."

"Thank you, sir. Aside from being becalmed for almost a week and weathering a terrible storm, the voyage was successful and uneventful."

Mr. Townsend nodded as John described the storm. "That must have been the hurricane that hit Wilmington on the Cape Fear River in the colony of North Carolina several weeks ago. Many buildings were destroyed, and the streets along the waterfront were flooded.

Several travelers who passed through here last week relayed the sad news. All we had here in Philadelphia was a lot of rain."

"That is terrible. You were fortunate that is all you had."

"Yes, we were. I would be pleased to provide you and your family with lodging. We have a spacious room available on the second floor that I believe you will find very comfortable. Please gather the rest of your family, and I will be happy to show you to that room."

"Thank you, sir. You are very kind. We shall return shortly with my family," John replied as he and Francis turned toward the front door. Then, pausing, he looked back at Mr. Townsend. "We have had a porter carry our belongings from the ship. There are several large chests, some furniture, and a box of tools. Can you suggest a place where they can be stored temporarily?"

"There is a large room at the back of the building where those items can be stored. You can ask the porter to take them there. I can also have my man, James, bring in any luggage you may have."

"Thank you, sir. Yes, I have one chest that needs to be delivered to the room, and I will instruct the porter about the other items. I will return shortly so you can show us our room."

As John and Francis stepped outside, the man with the horse-drawn cart carrying John's belongings was waiting.

"Please unload that smaller brown chest here and take the rest of the items around back to a room where they will be stored," John said.

"I will ensure the items are properly stored in the back room. That will be four pounds, sir."

John handed the man the requested amount. "Thank you, sir." Then, turning to Eliza, who was sitting on the bench with the other boys, John said, "They have a room for us, and Mr. Townsend, the proprietor, is ready to take us to it."

Eliza stood up, holding Matthew. "Wonderful!" Then, turning to Francis, she added, "Francis, please help George and Jack up the steps."

As they entered through the front door, Mr. Townsend was waiting for them.

"Eliza, may I present Mr. Jonathan Townsend, the proprietor? He will show us to our room," John said.

Eliza bowed her head toward Jonathan Townsend, saying, "It is a pleasure to meet you, sir."

Mr. Townsend nodded. "The pleasure is mine, Eliza."

"Mr. Townsend, you have met Francis. These are my other children: Jack, George, and Matthew," John said, pointing to each of the boys as he named them.

"You have a delightful family, sir!"

"Thank you, sir."

Mr. Townsend turned toward the stairs. "Now, if you follow me, I will show you to your room."

They all turned right at the top of the stairs and walked down a long hallway, stopping at a door on the right. Mr. Townsend opened the door to the room and handed John a key. "Here is your room, sir."

The large room had two windows on the opposite wall, with a door between them that opened onto a porch overlooking the harbor. In the twilight, the masts of several tall ships were visible, and Front Street glowed with candles shining through the windows of some shops. The furnishings included two simple double beds covered with quilted bedspreads made of Indian chintz, a basic six-drawer dresser with candles on top, a nightstand between the beds topped with a candle, and a secretary-style desk tucked into the far corner. The pine floorboards were covered with a well-worn tapestry rug, and a portrait of King George II hung on the wall between the beds.

As they entered the room, Mr. Townsend said, "Your chest should be delivered shortly. If there is anything that you need, please call on me."

John bowed to Mr. Townsend. "Thank you, sir."

After Mr. Townsend left, Eliza turned to John. "It's been a long day. I am famished, and the children are all hungry. Can we go downstairs and have supper before we settle in for the night?"

Francis chimed in, "That sounds like an excellent idea! I'm starving!"

John tossed his hat onto the bed. "It *has* been a long day and a long voyage. I'm hungry too! Let's go have supper."

Downstairs, the family gathered around a table in the dining area and took their seats. A waiter approached and introduced himself: "Good evening, sir. My name is Thomas. May I offer you and your family something to eat? We have roast pork or chicken tonight, accompanied by a variety of vegetables. We also have flounder with fried potatoes. Tonight's dessert is apple pie."

"Good evening, Thomas," John said. Then, turning to Eliza, he asked, "What sounds good to you, Eliza?"

Eliza, who was holding Matthew, replied, "The roast pork and vegetables sound wonderful."

"I would like some apple pie!" Francis exclaimed.

"We will have the roast pork and vegetables, Thomas," John said. Then he added, "And apple pie for dessert."

"Excellent choice, sir," Thomas replied before turning to head back to the kitchen.

When the food arrived, John offered a prayer of thanks for the meal and their safe journey on the ship before they started eating. Eliza placed some of her food on plates in front of Jack and George before taking a bite from her own plate.

"This is so good! It's been a long time since we've had a decent meal!" Eliza exclaimed.

"Yes, it is good!" Francis said as he took a bite of pork, the juices bursting on his tongue. "But I'm looking forward to the apple pie!" he said as the aroma of cinnamon wafted from the kitchen, promising a sweet end to the meal.

After they finished eating, including the apple pie, John stood up and said to Eliza, "Why don't you go back to the room to get the children settled and get some rest? I think I will head to the bar to meet some men there."

"Very well. I am exhausted," Eliza replied as she gathered the children and headed upstairs while John walked to the bar.

Candles decorated the tables in the barroom, and candleholders with candles were mounted on the walls. Some men sat at the tables, while others stood in front of the bar at the back of the room, drinking from pewter tankards. Behind the bar, a counter held several oak barrels, each with taps on the front, and bottles of whiskey and port.

John approached the bar just as the bartender was wiping it down with a towel. "What will it be, sir?" the bartender asked.

"I shall have an ale, please, sir."

"Excellent, sir," the bartender replied as he turned and filled a tankard.

"Excuse me, sir, ye must be new 'ere. Ah 'aven' seen 'e 'ere 'afore," said a man with a strong Scottish accent standing beside John.

"Yes, I have recently arrived from Ireland on the ship Dragon. And you are obviously from Scotland, sir. Have you been in Philadelphia long?" John replied, sipping from his tankard.

"Ay, sir, ahm from Edinburgh. A've been in Philadelphia three months noo. Ma name is James McLeod. To whom do I 'ave the 'onor o' speakin?" the man said.

"I am John Locke. It is a pleasure to meet you, James."

James bowed his head. "The pleasure's aw mine."

John sipped his ale. "I am staying here at the Blue Anchor with my family until I can find a permanent place to stay. Do you know anyone looking to take in boarders?"

"Ahm stayin' at a 'ouse at 100 Secon' Street, on the corner o Walnut Street, only a few blocks from 'ere. Thar are sev'ral boarders i' th' 'ouse, but a believe thare are still a few rooms left. Mrs. Charlotte Walker, wha owns th' 'ouse, is a wida'. The monthly rent also includes two meals a day, breakfas' an' supper."

"Thank you, sir. I will inquire there tomorrow. It was nice meeting you," John said as he finished his ale, placed three pence on the bar, and turned to leave.

Just then, Captain Hargrave walked up to the bar next to John. "Can I buy you another ale, Mr. Locke?"

"Hello, Captain! No, this one's on me for a successful voyage!"

"Thank you, sir!"

The bartender slid two tankards of ale across the bar to the men, who then took seats at a nearby table. The two men sat together, drinking their ale and talking.

John, reflecting on his conversation with Jonathan, said, "Jonathan Townsend mentioned to me that Wilmington, in the colony of North Carolina, was hit hard by that storm we encountered. Several buildings were destroyed, and the streets along the waterfront were flooded."

The captain set his tankard on the table and leaned back in his chair. "Yes, I heard that from some folks while walking along the dock. We are fortunate that the storm didn't move further north, or we could have been in trouble. How are Eliza and the children? I assume you've secured a room here."

"They are all tired but doing well. We have a very nice room. Eliza and the children are resting there now."

"Do you plan on staying in Philadelphia or moving somewhere else?"

"For now, we'll remain here in Philadelphia. I just spoke with that Scotsman at the bar," John said, pointing to James McLoud. "He told me about a boarding house nearby, and I'll inquire there tomorrow. Eventually, I plan to buy a house or land and build one."

"I wish you well here in the colonies, Mr. Locke," the captain said, finishing his ale and setting the tankard on the table. "I should head back to the ship. It's getting late, and I have an early start tomorrow, making sure the crew repairs the main mast and begins loading the cargo for the return voyage. Thank you for the ale!"

John also finished his ale and placed the empty tankard on the table. "You are very welcome, sir. I hope you get that mast repaired in short order and have a safe voyage back to Ireland."

The two friends left the bar together. Captain Hargrave returned to the ship while John retired to his room.

◆ ◆ ◆

During breakfast the next morning, John told Eliza about James McLeod's recommendation for a boarding house. After breakfast, Eliza took the children back to their room, and John walked down Front Street along the docks, turned right onto Walnut Street, and walked one block to Second Street. There, he found the boarding house that James McLeod had recommended. A sign above the door read Walker Boarding House.

He knocked on the door, and a middle-aged woman with graying hair pulled back in a bun greeted him. She wore a print skirt that reached her ankles, black leather shoes, and a tan blouse covered by a light blue linen apron. John removed his hat and bowed his head.

"Good morning, madam. My name is John Locke. I arrived yesterday on a ship from Belfast. I am here to inquire about the availability of a room for my family."

"Good morning, Mr. Locke. My name is Charlotte Walker. Please come in. We can discuss your needs, and I will show you around."

John entered the house and was led into the parlor, where they both sat down.

"Tell me about your family, Mr. Locke."

"I have a wife and four children, aged two to nine. We are temporarily staying at the Blue Anchor Tavern, where I met Mr. James McLeod last night. He told me about your establishment and suggested you have rooms available. Given the size of my family, I would like two adjoining rooms, if possible."

"Ah, Mr. McLeod is one of my tenants. He is a fine gentleman. I have one vacant room now, but I will have two adjoining rooms available next week."

"That would be wonderful! What do you charge?"

"The monthly rate is four pounds per room, paid on the first of the month. That includes a room with two beds and furniture, candles, weekly cleaning, and two meals per day—breakfast and supper. However, with four children, I will have to charge an additional pound per room to cover their meals."

"That would be satisfactory. Do you need a deposit?"

"No deposit is necessary. You may plan to move in next Monday. Would you like to see a room and tour the house?"

"Yes, I would, thank you."

After he viewed the room and toured the house, John returned to his room at the Blue Anchor Tavern.

"We have two adjoining rooms at the Walker Boarding House beginning next Monday," John said to Eliza as he entered their room.

Eliza was feeding Matthew while the other children lounged on the beds. "Wonderful! Is it very far from here?"

"Only a few blocks. The proprietor, Mrs. Walker, is very nice. The rooms are large, and each comes with two beds, furniture, candles, weekly cleaning, and breakfast and supper each day."

"That sounds good. It will be nice to have more space," Eliza replied as she finished feeding Matthew.

Francis, clearly bored, jumped off the bed and asked, "Can we take a walk and see some of the city?"

"That would be nice!" Eliza replied.

"Absolutely!" John said.

The family spent the day exploring Philadelphia, taking in the sights and enjoying the cool fall weather. They even stopped at the confectionery shop to get a treat for the children.

4

A Chance Meeting

In 1726, five years before John and Eliza Locke arrived in America, Richard Brandon and his wife, Mary, emigrated from London and eventually settled in Lancaster, about 80 miles west of Philadelphia. Neither the Brandons nor the Lockes realized at the time that the Brandons' move to America and their later relocation to Lancaster would be a key event for both families.

By 1731, the Brandons had established a home on 20 acres near Lancaster. The house featured white-painted clapboard siding, three bedrooms, a living room with a fireplace, and a spacious kitchen with a second fireplace for cooking. There was a barn with two horse stalls, a henhouse, and a smokehouse behind the house. They had a horse, a cow, and several hogs, and Mary enjoyed tending the vegetable garden and gathering eggs from the henhouse.

"I love our home!" Mary exclaimed. "I am so glad we moved out of the hustle and bustle of the city."

"Yes, Philadelphia was getting too crowded. It is so much nicer here!" Richard replied.

"And the children have lots of friends here, and they have room to play outside," Mary added.

One evening in September, Richard stopped by the Hickory Tree Tavern near his home and was greeted by George Gibson, the proprietor.

"Good evening, Richard. I hope you are well today!"

"Good evening, George. Yes, all is well, and the family is doing fine. May I have a beer, please?"

"Yes, sir," George said as he finished serving a man beside Richard. Then he added, "Richard, allow me to introduce you to a new arrival in our fair town, Christiaan Janson. Christiaan has recently arrived from Amsterdam with his family. Christian, this is Richard Brandon."

Richard bowed toward Christiaan. "Good evening, Mr. Janson.

Welcome to Lancaster. I trust you had a pleasant voyage and have found a suitable place to live."

The voyage went smoothly, and yes, my wife, Emma, and I are currently staying with friends. But we don't plan to stay here long: I'm a farmer, so we're planning to move to the colony of North Carolina, where land is cheap.

Richard sipped his beer. "I've heard tales of cheap land in North Carolina, but I've also heard that the journey there is difficult and dangerous. There's a road—if you can call it that—that runs from here through Pennsylvania, Virginia, the Carolinas, and into Georgia, known as the Great Wagon Road or the Great Warrior's Path. It follows a route the Indians have used for centuries."

Christiaan set his tankard of beer on the bar. "I am familiar with the stories of those who have traveled that road and the challenges they faced. However, the reward is substantial for those willing to endure the hardships. My brother successfully moved his family to North Carolina last year, and we plan to settle near his farm in Anson County. He has written to me, describing Anson County as a place where land is both affordable and highly fertile. The climate is not as cold as here, and the landscape is rolling hills and meadows. There are abundant hardwood forests for lumber to build a home."

"You have given me much to think about, sir, and I wish you a safe journey and much success in North Carolina," Richard replied. "Permit me to buy you another beer to toast your arrival in America."

"Thank you, sir. That would be most agreeable."

The two men sat at a table while Christiaan continued to share details about North Carolina with Richard.

The next morning, as Richard sat at the kitchen table while Mary prepared breakfast, he remembered his conversations with Christiaan from the night before. "I met a man from Amsterdam named Christiaan last night at the tavern. He gave me a lot to think about. He plans to travel south along the Great Wagon Road to the colony of North Carolina. He said his brother is near the Irish Settlement in Anson County. The land is plentiful and cheap, and the climate is very agreeable. We might want to move there someday."

"It will require a lot of planning and saving, and we have a nice home here. I hope you're not considering that!" Mary exclaimed.

"It's something to think about. What's for breakfast?"

Mary placed a frying pan on the grate above the cooking fire. "I am frying up some of that ham from the smokehouse and some fresh eggs I gathered earlier this morning from the henhouse."

"Wonderful! I'm hungry!"

As the family sat around the table enjoying breakfast, Mary said, "Richard, we need a few things for the house that I cannot find in shops here. Can you take the wagon to Philadelphia sometime next week?"

"Yes, I can plan on going on Monday. I will have to stay for several nights, since it takes almost a day to travel each way, and I'm sure I will need a day to shop. What do you need?"

Mary took a bite of ham. "The children need new shoes, and I need fabric to make clothes for them and curtains. We need new plates and cups since some are broken and several are chipped. We could also use another kitchen table. I'm afraid that this old table has seen its last days. I'm sure you won't remember everything, so I will make a list."

"I will plan on getting an early start on Monday, staying at the Blue Anchor Tavern for two nights, and returning on Wednesday. It will be nice to see Jonathan Townsend again and catch up on the latest news."

"I'll pack some bread, cheese, and dried meat for you in a basket for the trip," Mary offered.

"That would be great!" Richard replied as he finished his breakfast and stood up.

◆◆◆

Before sunrise on Monday morning, Richard hitched the horse to the wagon, checked the wheels and undercarriage for damage, and greased the wheel bearings while Mary prepared the basket of food for their trip. By daybreak, he was on his way to Philadelphia.

The road between Lancaster and Philadelphia was well-maintained, with many travelers on foot, horseback, or riding in wagons. Richard arrived in Philadelphia as the sun was setting and pulled the wagon up to the front of the Blue Anchor Tavern. He engaged the brake, jumped down from the wagon, and walked through the front door.

"Good evening, Jonathan," Richard said as he entered the bar.

"Good to see you again, Richard. What brings you to Philadelphia?"

"Good to see you, too, Jonathan. I need to pick up a few things for Mary, and I also need a few things. I will need to stay for several nights. Do you have a room available?"

"Of course I do, for an old friend."

"That would be very nice, thank you. My wagon is outside. May I unhitch my horse and lead him into one of your stalls in the barn?"

"Just pull your wagon around back. My man, James, will unhitch your horse, put him in a stall, and feed and water him."

"Thank you, sir. I shall return shortly, and I could use a glass of port. It has been a long day on the road," Richard said as he turned and headed for the door.

When Richard returned to the tavern, the sun had set, and the stars were out. Men were talking, laughing, and drinking as he stepped into the barroom. As Richard approached the bar, Jonathan poured him a glass of port.

Richard nodded, picked up the glass, and lifted it to his lips. "Thank you, sir."

"You are welcome. Here is the key to your room."

After finishing his port and feeling tired from his journey, Richard retired to his room for the night.

◆ ◆ ◆

The next morning after breakfast, Richard spent the day visiting several shops to buy the items Mary had listed. After he pulled his loaded wagon to the back of the tavern, unhitched his horse, and led it into a stall, he entered the tavern and approached the bar.

"Good evening, Jonathan. May I please have a beer?"

"Yes, sir, coming up," Jonathan replied. "How was your day? Were you able to purchase the items you needed?"

"I got everything I was sent for and a few things I needed, too."

Jonathan filled a tankard with beer and placed it on the bar in front of Richard. "Good. Now, you can relax before heading back to Lancaster tomorrow."

"Yes, and I will need to start early tomorrow to get home before dark," Richard said as he lifted the tankard to his lips.

Just then, John Locke walked up to the bar. "Good evening, Jonathan. I trust all is well with you. May I have a beer, please?"

"Yes, you may," Jonathan replied.

As Jonathan set a tankard in front of John, he nodded toward Richard. "Permit me to introduce Mr. Richard Brandon from Lancaster, about 80 miles west of here. Richard, this is John Locke, who recently arrived here with his family from Ireland."

"Good evening, sir. It is a pleasure to meet you," John said, bowing his head. "I have heard of Lancaster. Isn't there a large Amish community there?"

"Yes. The Amish are very industrious and peaceful citizens in our little town. Also, housing is cheap and available in Lancaster because many families are selling to move south to the Virginia and Carolina colonies," Richard said. "Are you staying here at the Blue Anchor Tavern?"

"I am staying here with my wife and children for now. Today, I inquired about a boarding house here in the city. Two rooms will be available for my family next week. We will stay there until I can find a suitable home here in the city."

Richard placed his beer on the bar, feeling the need to share some advice. "Because of the significant influx of people from England, Ireland, Scotland, and Europe to Philadelphia, housing here has become very expensive, and the city is rapidly becoming overcrowded. You may want to consider buying property outside the city, such as in Lancaster. Lancaster is a charming little town, much nicer than living in a busy, crowded city like Philadelphia. We moved there five years ago, and we love it."

John nodded and raised his glass to take a sip. "Thank you, sir, for that recommendation. I will discuss that with my wife. Tell me more about Lancaster."

The two men sat at a table in the tavern for several hours, discussing life in Lancaster compared to Philadelphia, their families, and the latest news from England. By the end of the evening, they had developed a close friendship, and John had decided to settle his young family in Lancaster.

◆ ◆ ◆

It was late when John returned to his room, excited about his conversation with Richard. He sat on the bed beside Eliza, who was feeding Matthew while the other children slept. "I just met a man in the tavern who got me thinking."

"Oh? About what?" Eliza asked.

While Eliza listened patiently, John described his conversation with Richard, explaining how they shared similar values and outlooks on life and how he extolled the benefits of living in Lancaster versus Philadelphia.

Eliza finished feeding Matthew, placed him on the bed, and shrugged as she thought, *We have just arrived in Philadelphia today and haven't even settled into a permanent residence. Now, he is talking about relocating?*

"It sounds very nice, John, but finding a suitable home in Lancaster and moving there may take a while. Besides, we just arrived today. Can we think about this some more?" she replied.

"I know. We can stay at the boarding house until we decide what to do. Richard has invited us to visit them over Christmas to see if we would like Lancaster. From the way he talked, they are just like us. They have children about the same age as ours. They are from London."

Eliza reclined against a pillow and sighed. "It would be nice to have some close friends here in Pennsylvania. I'm missing my family and friends back home. But a move so soon?"

John smiled. "I know. I miss my family and friends too. Once we get settled in the boarding house, I will write to him to find out when it would be convenient to visit them in Lancaster."

"Fine," Eliza said. "That will give us time to adjust to Philadelphia and discuss this further."

With that said, and hearing her say, "Fine," John knew not to push it any further. Still, he was determined to move to Lancaster one day. He changed into his nightshirt and nightcap, slipped into bed, kissed Eliza goodnight, and fell asleep within minutes, exhausted from the day's events.

5
Lancaster

The Lockes visited the Brandons later that year over the Christmas holidays. Then, throughout the spring and early summer of 1732, they stayed with the Brandons several times while they searched for property in Lancaster. With every visit, their common backgrounds and experiences drew the families closer together.

On one such trip, John discovered a house that he believed Eliza would adore. It was a single-story brick structure on the outskirts of Lancaster. It featured a large kitchen with a stone fireplace, three bedrooms, and a spacious living area with an additional fireplace. The ten-acre lot featured a small barn at the back, complete with two horse stalls and a small tack room. Next to the barn, there was a fenced pasture on one side and a tool shed on the other side with an attached chicken coop behind it.

As they entered the house, Eliza roamed from room to room, admiring each space, especially the spacious kitchen with its fireplace, which was perfect for cooking.

"Oh, John, this house is amazing! Please buy it!"

"I agree," John replied. "It is a very nice home in which to raise our family. I will make an offer today."

It was the perfect home for the Lockes' growing family, and John acquired it at a reasonable price. By early November, the family had moved in and settled into their new home, and John had acquired a horse, a few hens, and a rooster.

One day, there was a knock at the door. When John opened the door, the Brandons were standing there and exclaimed in unison: "Welcome to Lancaster!"

John welcomed them into their new home with open arms. "Please come in! We are so delighted to have been blessed with this property."

Then, handing Eliza a set of hand-stitched dish towels, Mary said, "Here is a little housewarming gift for you, Eliza."

"Thank you so much, Mary! These are just what I needed!"

While the men and older boys went to the barn to feed the horse and chickens, the younger children played, and the two women sat around the kitchen table talking as Eliza poured them a cup of tea.

"You're all invited back here next week to celebrate our move to Lancaster and to give thanks for how our families have been blessed. I will be cooking a turkey that John shot yesterday."

"I can bring a ham from our smokehouse and some sweet potatoes and collards from our garden," Mary offered.

Eliza continued to admire the handmade dish towels. "Oh, that would be wonderful, and I can bake a pumpkin pie!"

On the appointed day, the Brandons arrived with their three children, ages nineteen to seven. The Locke children, who ranged in age from ten to two, were thrilled to have other children to play with. While the women prepared the meal in the kitchen, the men and older boys played cricket in the pasture, and the younger children enjoyed playing hide-and-seek, tag, and hopscotch outside.

When the food was ready, the families gathered together, and John offered a prayer of thanks for God's blessings. The turkey was carved, the ham sliced, and the men and older boys helped themselves while the women prepared plates for the younger children and themselves. This initial gathering of the Brandon and Locke families to give thanks for life's many blessings became a cherished tradition, symbolizing their unity and shared values.

One evening in 1736, John and Richard sat in the Hickory Tree Tavern discussing politics. As often occurs, the conversation shifted to grievances concerning taxation and the actions of the government.

"Richard, I think you should run for the County Assessor position in Hanover County in the upcoming election," John said as he took a sip of beer.

"Why? I know nothing about collecting taxes."

"You're good with money and honest. Those are the most important qualities. Besides, there are rumors that the current tax assessor is stepping down, and you are well respected, so your election would be a certainty."

"I will give it some thought," Richard replied, finishing his beer and standing. "It's late. I need to be heading home."

"It *is* late. Eliza will wonder where I am," John said as he stood. "If you decide to run for office, you will have my full support."

"Hello, dear. I'm home," Richard said as he entered his house and saw that Mary was sitting by the fireplace, knitting.

She stood and greeted her husband with a kiss. "Good. It's late, and I was worried about you."

"I had an interesting discussion with John at the tavern this evening," Richard began as they sat down by the fireplace.

"Oh? About what?"

"Mostly politics. John thinks I should run for County Assessor in Hanover Township."

Mary didn't look up, and she didn't miss a stitch as she continued her knitting and thought about what Richard had said.

Richard continued, "The current Tax Assessor is stepping down, so John thinks my election would be a certainty."

Mary laid down her knitting and looked at her husband. "Why would you want to run for that office? Are you even qualified?"

"I think I might enjoy serving the county, and it would give me a chance to get out and meet people. And yes, I am good at handling money, and I'm honest. Those are the primary qualifications."

"What are the duties of a County Assessor?"

"Mainly collecting taxes. John thinks I would be perfect for the position."

"If that's what you want to do, then you have my blessing," Mary assured him. "It's late. Are you ready to go to bed?"

"Yes, I am. It's been a long day."

The next day, Richard asked John to be his campaign manager. John agreed, and for the next two months, the two distributed flyers, shook hands, and knocked on doors throughout the township and county.

Elections took place in early October, and Richard was elected by a large margin, as announced in the *Pennsylvania Gazette*. Richard served honorably as the County Assessor of Hanover Township for several years.

◆ ◆ ◆

In December 1742, the Locke family had been living in Lancaster for ten years, and Francis turned 20.

"Happy birthday, son! We couldn't be prouder of the person you've become," John beamed.

"Thank you, Father," Francis replied, his voice filled with pride.

As the two families gathered around the Brandon kitchen table, Mary presented a cake, and they all wished Francis a happy birthday.

"Here's a birthday present for you," John said as he presented Francis with a new Pennsylvania long rifle.

Francis immediately took the rifle, shouldered it, and aimed it out the window. "Thank you, Father! It is beautiful! I cannot wait to try it out."

"Maybe now you will get that ten-point buck down by the creek you missed last week!" John joked with a broad grin.

Embarrassed by that comment, Francis rolled his eyes, grinned, and shook his head as everyone laughed.

Richard handed Francis a gift. "Happy birthday, Francis. We have watched you grow from a boy into a man and we are so proud of you! Here's a new powder horn that I made for you. You will need it if you plan on shooting that buck!"

"Thank you, sir! I can certainly make use of that!"

The families continued to enjoy the cake and tease Francis a bit more.

Mary, who was due to give birth any day, suddenly placed her plate on the table, her face twisted in pain. "Oh my, I'm having some labor pains! I think it's time for the baby to come."

Eliza immediately took Mary's arm and led her to the bedroom. "Come with me, dear." Then, speaking over her shoulder to her husband, "John, please put a pot of water on to boil, and we will need some clean towels."

Eliza assisted Mary as she labored for several hours while the men prayed and looked after the younger children.

By nightfall, a baby's cry was heard, and Mary had given birth to a baby girl. Eliza emerged from the bedroom, cradling the newborn wrapped in a receiving blanket.

She gently placed the baby into Richard's arms and announced, "Richard, here is your new daughter."

"She's beautiful!" he exclaimed as he admired his newborn daughter.

"Mary and I have already chosen a name for her: Hannah. How is Mary doing?"

"She is exhausted and resting. But I am sure she would like to see you."

Richard headed toward the bedroom with his newborn daughter in his arms. As he stepped into the bedroom, he saw Mary lying in bed. She lifted her head and smiled weakly as he cradled their newborn daughter in his arms.

"She's perfect!" he exclaimed. "How are you feeling?"

Mary's voice was weary. "I'm fine. I'm just tired, and I feel very weak. It was a difficult delivery."

In the kitchen, Eliza turned to her husband, her eyes filled with concern. "John, I'm deeply worried about Mary. She had a hard labor, and she is still experiencing some bleeding. I should stay with her overnight to make sure she is alright."

"No problem. I will take the children home and tuck them in bed tonight."

Eliza stayed with Mary throughout the night. By dawn, her condition had not improved—she was still bleeding, experiencing severe abdominal pain, and beginning to run a fever.

Richard looked at his son, James, with concern. "Richard, your mother has not recovered from the birth, and I am afraid that she may not make it. Saddle the horse and ride to fetch Doctor Neff."

When the doctor arrived, Richard greeted him at the door. "Come in, Doc. My wife has just given birth to a baby girl. The baby is fine, but my wife is not doing well. She is still bleeding, and she has a fever."

The doctor examined Mary and then took Richard aside, a concerned expression on his face. "She is experiencing internal bleeding from the birth, and she has a fever, likely caused by retained afterbirth tissue. I am so sorry, but I can do nothing. She may not make it if her body cannot fight this. She must stay in bed, and you should keep her as cool as possible with wet towels on her forehead. I will check on her again tomorrow."

On the morning of New Year's Day, 1743, Richard greeted the doctor at the door as he arrived. "Come in, Doc. I'm afraid her condition is worse. Although the bleeding has almost stopped, her fever is now very high, and she is not responsive."

The doctor applied leeches to Mary's abdomen. "Keep wet towels on her and open a window to let the cold air cool her."

By late afternoon, with Mary's condition still not improving, the doctor removed the leeches. "Keep her as cool as possible. There is not much more I can do here today. I will come again tomorrow to check on her."

That evening, Mary opened her eyes and slowly reached out to touch her husband's hand. "Richard, I am so weak, and I feel I will soon be in the presence of our Lord. Please take care of the children, especially baby Hannah. And remember that I have always loved you."

With that, she closed her eyes and took her last breath.

Mary Brandon, age 52, passed away with her husband, Richard, and her children by her side. The funeral, held at the First Presbyterian Church in Lancaster, was a small, intimate affair. Mary had been a loving wife and mother and had lived a full life. Her devoted husband, Richard, their children, the Lockes, and a few close friends were in attendance. The simple wooden casket was draped with a white linen cloth, and a single red rose rested on top of it.

As the minister spoke, Richard broke down and sobbed uncontrollably as thoughts ran through his head. *I already miss her smile and loving touch. Why did this have to happen? What will I do without her, and how can I possibly care for the children, especially baby Hannah?*

She was the love of his life, filling his days with immense joy. As he looked around the room, he noticed the tears in everyone's eyes and realized they, too, shared his profound sorrow. She was gone, but he would forever remember her beauty, kindness, and quiet strength.

After Mary's death, Eliza assumed responsibility for caring for the Brandon children, especially baby Hannah, as well as her own children. There were three Brandon children under 18, and Eliza had four. While Eliza and the older girls attended to the younger children, the men and older boys spent their time hunting, fishing, performing daily chores, and caring for the livestock, which now included several horses and cows, a few pigs, and many chickens and ducks.

By early 1744, Richard had finally moved past Mary's death, even though her memory still haunted him daily, especially when he held baby Hannah.

"She has her mother's eyes and smile," Richard confided to Eliza one day. "I can't look at her without thinking of Mary."

In the spring, Richard purchased a 250-acre farm in West Hanover Township and worked on it throughout the summer and fall, assisted by John and Francis.

The families had plenty to eat that summer. Francis had become skilled with his Pennsylvania long rifle, providing venison, rabbits, and turkeys. The farm also yielded a large crop of vegetables. Eliza and the girls even preserved some of the corn, beans, okra, and tomatoes, and they pickled cucumbers.

One October morning at dawn, John and Francis Locke were preparing to go to the farm to harvest pumpkins. Between coughing and wheezing, John told Francis, "I'm not feeling well, so I'm going back to bed; you go on without me today."

When Francis returned from the farm at sunset, he found his father coughing, wheezing, and sweating profusely in bed. Eliza had been caring for him throughout the day, but his condition had worsened.

Francis looked at him with concern. "Father, you're not well. I'm going to fetch Dr. Neef."

"Wait until tomorrow morning. If I am not better, you can fetch the doctor."

By dawn the following day, John was coughing, gasping for air, perspiring heavily, and running a dangerously high fever. Francis rushed to the barn, saddled a horse, and rode to fetch Dr. Neef.

When Francis and the doctor returned and entered the bedroom, Eliza, sitting on the bed beside her husband and holding his hand, looked up. "Doctor, I am afraid he is not well," Eliza said, concern showing in her eyes.

"Please wait outside while I examine him," the doctor requested.

After examining John between his fits of coughing and wheezing, the doctor walked into the kitchen, where Eliza and Francis were. "I am afraid there is nothing I can do. Your husband has consumption. Just keep him comfortable and try to get him to eat some soup. I will check back again tomorrow," the doctor sighed.

The next morning, Eliza was sitting on the bed beside her husband when the doctor arrived.

She looked up as the doctor entered the room, and with tears in her eyes, her only words were, "He's gone."

John Locke, aged 44, had passed away peacefully with his loving wife, Eliza, at his side. The family, the Brandons, and the many friends he had made attended the funeral at the First Presbyterian Church in Lancaster.

After his father's passing, Francis Locke, 22, the eldest son, posted an administrative bond for his widowed mother, as required by law, and took on the role of head of the household.

In late November, Francis and Richard were splitting and stacking firewood outside the barn for the coming winter.

Richard split a log, put his axe down, and looked at Francis. "Francis, I need to ask you something."

"What?" Francis asked as he placed another log on the chopping block and lifted his axe.

Richard sat down on a log, wiped the sweat off his brow, and took a deep breath. "Since your father's passing, your mother and I have grown very close. As the head of your household, with your permission and blessing, I would like to ask for her hand in marriage."

Francis laid his axe down and looked at Richard for a long time, trying to decide how to answer. He had seen how his mother looked at Richard and even glimpsed them holding hands one evening as they walked toward the barn.

"Sir, you have been like a father to me since my father's death, and Mother has been caring for your children since your wife passed away."

Francis paused momentarily and took a deep breath. "I have no objection to your marrying my mother. You have my blessing."

Richard let out a sigh of relief. "Thank you, Francis. That means a lot to me, but I would marry her even without your blessing!"

Francis rolled his eyes. "I do not doubt that!"

In December 1744, Richard Brandon and Eliza Locke married in a quiet ceremony at the First Presbyterian Church of Lancaster. Reverend Richard Woodhull officiated, and the wedding was attended by all their children and a few close friends.

As Eliza prepared breakfast for the family one morning in 1747, Richard said, "Many years ago, I met a man from Amsterdam named Christiaan Janson who shared something that I often think about. He planned to travel along the Great Wagon Road to the colony of North Carolina. He said that the land there is abundant and affordable. Pennsylvania is becoming increasingly crowded because of the influx of families from Europe. I'm thinking that we should eventually move to North Carolina."

Eliza placed a plate of flapjacks and sausage before her husband. "Richard, we have a good life here, and the children are all happy and well. Do you *really* wish to uproot the family for such a perilous journey?"

Richard took a bite of sausage. "The man also mentioned that the climate in the Carolinas is far more agreeable than here in Pennsylvania. Winters are milder there, with not nearly as much snow and ice as in Pennsylvania."

"Winters here *are* harsh. It would be nice to live somewhere warmer. I'll think about it, but knowing you, you'll do what you want to do, anyway!"

James was sitting at the table, waiting for his breakfast. "I've heard similar stories, but I've also heard that the journey along the Great Wagon Road is long and dangerous."

Hearing the conversation, Francis entered the kitchen and sat at the table. "I've heard of several families who have journeyed south. They've written to relatives here in Lancaster, saying North Carolina is a wonderful place to live."

"The British have imposed more and more economic restrictions and introduced new taxes upon us here in Pennsylvania over the past decade," Richard interjected. "Many families are moving to North Carolina to escape British oppression and high taxes."

"That's a valid argument," Eliza answered.

Richard continued, "If we sell all of our properties, including the farm, we should have enough money to purchase the wagons and supplies for the trip, plus enough to purchase land when we arrive in North Carolina. Also, I have heard that some men have received land grants in North Carolina from the Earl of Granville."

Eliza served James and Francis their breakfast. "It sounds like you have already decided, Richard. Fine, I will agree, but only if we have the resources and a plan for this move."

The family continued eating breakfast and talking about North Carolina. By the end of the meal, Eliza was on board with the idea, and Richard was more determined than ever to move his family to North Carolina.

6
The Great Wagon Road

By late summer 1748, Richard and Eliza Brandon, along with their adult children and stepchildren, had spent months planning and preparing for their long journey down the Great Wagon Road. Richard arranged for the sale of their property, as well as any personal items and furniture they wouldn't take on the trip.

The four oldest sons—Richard Brandon Jr., who was called Rick, 35, James Brandon, 33, Francis Locke, 26, and William Brandon, 22—acquired three sturdy Conestoga wagons and teams of oxen to pull them.

George and Matthew Locke assisted Eliza in gathering the provisions needed for the trip: sacks of flour and cornmeal, dried meat, and fruit, all carefully packed into barrels and crates. They packed axes, hammers, and saws, knowing these tools would be crucial for building new homes upon their arrival in North Carolina, and they also carried a few spare wagon wheels in case one needed replacing.

The grown men ensured they had enough gunpowder, flints, and lead for their firearms, while Eliza gathered extra fabric, needles, and thread to repair clothes along the way. Horses were shod, oxen were harnessed, and the wagons were reinforced for the rugged terrain ahead.

In the first week of September, the night before their departure, the family gathered to finalize their plans.

"We must stay together," Richard told the group. "The road is treacherous, and there is safety in numbers. The wagons are to stay close, and no one rides ahead alone."

Francis nodded. "William, James, and I can take turns standing watch at night. I've heard stories about bandits and Indian raiding parties. We'll be ready for them."

As dawn broke the next day, a cool, foggy morning greeted the wagons as they started out, their wheels groaning under their heavy loads. Richard flicked the reins, urging the oxen forward, while Eliza held six-year-old Hannah Brandon and four-year-old Elizabeth Locke close against the fall chill. Behind them, the wagons of several other families traveled in a tight formation as they rumbled down the narrow dirt road heading south. Several horses were tied to the back of the wagons.

Richard drove the lead wagon, followed by his eldest son, Rick, while George brought up the rear. Francis and Jack walked beside the wagons, muskets slung over their shoulders, keeping watch for unseen dangers. Unaware of the dangers ahead, the younger children were eager to embark on this adventure.

The road was rough, with deep ruts left by those who had passed before them. The wagons jolted over stones and tree roots, sending shudders through the wooden frames and the passengers. Inside the lead wagon, Eliza cautioned her stepdaughters, Mary and Anna, who were sitting beside her, "Hold on tight, girls! It's going to be a bumpy ride!"

◆◆◆

At midday, the group paused on the banks of the Susquehanna River to rest the oxen and enjoy a meal of bread, cheese, and dried apples. Nearby, other travelers ate, tended to their animals, and discussed the upcoming journey.

When they crossed the Susquehanna River, the water was flowing gently, and the riverbed was stable, about 50 feet wide and knee-deep. At each crossing, everyone except the drivers was required to get out of the wagons and walk across in case the wagon tipped over. This was especially important if the water was swift or deep.

As the sun set that evening, they picked a clearing near a small creek to camp for the night, close to the other families traveling with them. Francis shot and skinned some rabbits while the other men gathered firewood. With the fire blazing, the women prepared a simple meal of rabbit stew and cornbread. The rich aroma of cooking meat filled the cool night air as the children played nearby, their laughter providing a brief respite from the journey's challenges. Richard and Francis sat close to the fire, discussing the road ahead while keeping their muskets within easy reach.

With the embers fading from the dying fire and stars twinkling above, everyone went to bed, except Francis, who was on watch that night. He added another log to the fire and lay down in front of it on his blanket, his musket by his side.

About midnight, Anna quietly walked up, sat down beside him. "Hi, Francis!"

Startled, Francis quickly sat up. "Oh, hello, Anna. You surprised me!"

"I couldn't sleep, so I thought you might need some company."

"Yes, it gets lonely out here," Francis replied as they both sat close together on the blanket, enjoying the warmth of the fire and unsure of what to say.

Francis's mind raced. *I wonder if she really can't sleep? I have caught her occasionally looking at me and smiling. Maybe it's just an excuse to be with me! Does she have feelings for me? I know I'm attracted to her. She is beautiful! Should I try to kiss her? No! I shouldn't. She might not like it, or she might slap me! Or she might get up and leave. Or, worse, she might tell her father!*

Finally, Anna announced, "It's chillier out here than I expected."

"I can take care of that," Francis said, getting up and throwing another log on the fire.

As he sat back down, he said, "And maybe this will help, too," as he removed his coat and placed it around her shoulders.

"Thank you," Anna said, drawing the coat closer and enjoying its warmth, thinking, *That is so sweet of him to give me his coat! And it smells like him—kind of woodsy and manly. He touched my shoulders as he wrapped it around me! Oh, how I have longed for his touch! I have to admit, I think I could fall in love! I wonder how he feels about me? He must care about me, or he wouldn't have given me his coat! Will he try to kiss me, or should I dare to kiss him?*

The two sat there for a while, enjoying the warmth of the fire.

Finally, Francis said, "It *is* late. Don't you think you should go back to bed?"

"I'm not sleepy, and besides, I'm enjoying being with you," Anna replied dreamily as their eyes met.

As they sat there together, not knowing what else to say, Anna finally leaned back against a log and yawned.

"You *are* sleepy! You probably should go back to bed. We have an early start tomorrow. Besides, you don't need to be here alone with me. Somebody may see us," Francis said as he stood.

"If you insist," Anna replied.

Francis took her hand to help her stand, then he reached around her to remove his coat. When he did, she felt the warmth of his breath close to her face, and her knees became weak, having him touch her and his lips that close.

"Now go to bed," Francis said after putting his coat back on.

"Very well. Good night, Francis."

"Good night."

Anna returned to her bed in the wagon, but she couldn't sleep the rest of the night thinking about him.

The next morning, they had barely traveled a mile when a sharp crack rang out. Several spokes on the lead wagon's wheel had shattered as it rolled over a large tree root.

Richard knelt beside the wheel, running his fingers over the jagged breaks. "This will set us back half a day," he muttered, frustrated. "Luckily, we are carrying a spare wheel."

Looking at the damaged wagon wheel, Francis assured him, "At least we are on level ground and not on a steep hill. Let's get to work."

James and William gathered tools while Francis cut down a small tree to use as leverage for lifting the wagon. After the men unloaded the wagon, Francis placed the tree under the front axle near the broken wheel, and William assisted him in lifting the wagon, raising the wheel off the ground. Richard removed the damaged wheel and slid a new one onto the hub while Francis and William supported the wagon with the tree Francis had cut down.

While the men replaced the wheel and reloaded the wagon, the women took advantage of the delay by refilling the water barrels from a nearby stream.

As the group continued their journey, the further south they went, the more untamed the land became. Thick forests closed in on both sides of the road, and at night, they slept to the sounds of owls, whip-poor-wills, and the occasional howl of wolves. Richard, William, James, and Francis took turns sleeping by the fire and keeping watch throughout the night, their muskets within reach.

One evening, after the family finished supper and cleaned up, Richard and Francis went over to a nearby family's campsite.

"Good evening to you. How far will you be traveling?" Richard asked, approaching their campfire.

"Good evening, sirs. We are from Bethlehem in Pennsylvania, bound for Bethabara, the new Moravian settlement in North Carolina. The Lord has guided us thus far," Brother Matthias replied, bowing his head.

Francis eyed their wagons. "Your wagons are heavily loaded. What are you hauling?"

"We are taking supplies to the settlement—tools, cloth, and medicines. We also have Bibles and hymnals for our brethren."

"I am acquainted with several Moravians back in Lancaster. You are all hard workers, but not much for fighting," Richard said.

Upon hearing their conversation, Sister Ann, with a shawl over her shoulders, approached the group.

Francis tipped his hat. "Good evening, ma'am."

"Good evening to you, sir. We prefer to settle disputes peacefully, not through fighting."

Francis crossed his arms and thought for a moment. "That's fine, but peace does not last long out here. The Cherokee and other tribes grow restless, and they do not take kindly to settlers coming into their land."

"We trust in God to keep us safe. And where that is not enough, honesty and fair trade can ease many tensions," Brother Matthias offered.

Richard thought for a moment. "That may be, but a man's word will not always stop an arrow—or a musket ball."

Brother Samuel squatted by the fire and stirred the embers with a stick. "That is true, sir. But we do not seek confrontation. We offer our hands in labor and our hearts in prayer."

"Prayer is good, but a rifle's better when the time comes," Francis said, his hand resting on the pistol in his belt.

"We do not condemn those who take up arms in defense. But we chose a different path," Sister Ann gently stated.

Then, glancing at their wagons again, Francis asked, "Brother Mathias, what do you trade for your supplies?"

"Our people produce a diverse range of quality goods. At Bethabara, we create furniture and pottery. We operate a sawmill that produces boards and shingles for the construction trade. And we have a brewery where we brew beer and distill whiskey. We also bake fresh bread and make cheese in our settlement."

"Good cheese is rare. I might have to visit Bethabara," Francis said with a grin.

"You would be most welcome, sir."

"I may take you up on that offer one day," Francis replied, bowing his head toward Brother Matthias.

"Well, it was nice meeting you," Richard said. Then, looking at Francis, "We must be getting back to our camp. It's late, and we have an early start in the morning."

"Then may God bless your journey as He blesses ours," Sister Ann said, smiling. "And may He keep you safe, too."

"Good evening to you all," Francis said as he and Richard turned to leave.

By early October, they reached the Potomac River and were pleased to find a ferry operated by Philip Noland. The river, approximately 100 yards wide, presented a challenge. The ferry could transport only one wagon at a time, so the entire day was consumed in getting the convoy across. By the time the last wagon reached the other side, dusk was fast approaching, so the group camped there for the night. As several of the group sat on logs around the campfire that night, Francis said, "I am sure glad there was a ferry here."

"Yes. This river is very wide. And deep. We would have had a difficult time crossing without the ferry," Richard replied, poking the fire with a stick.

"How many more rivers will we have to cross?" Eliza asked.

Francis threw another log on the fire. "There are several more, but I do not think any will be as wide as this one."

"I think the only river that will pose any difficulty for us will be the Yadkin River in North Carolina," Richard said.

"I have heard that heavy rains upstream can cause it to swell and flow fast."

"Well," Eliza said. "If that's the only one we have trouble with, then I'll be happy."

"I am more concerned about the possibility of bandits or Indians than I am about crossing a river," Francis said.

"I agree," William said. "But if we are attacked, we will be ready for them."

As the fire died down, everyone turned in for the night, except for Francis and Richard, who stayed by the fire keeping watch. Francis added another log to the fire and settled in with his musket by his side, while Richard leaned against a log and slept.

Around midnight, a rustling and grunting noise near one wagon startled him, so he got up to investigate. Creeping around the back of the wagon and seeing nothing, he moved to the far side, tightening the grip on his musket. When Francis neared the front of the wagon, he could barely make out in the dim light from the distant campfire a large shape with black fur about 30 feet away, tearing into a food box left near the wagon tongue. It was a big, black bear. Taking a careful step toward the bear, Francis accidentally stepped on a stick, alerting the animal. It immediately whirled around, stood on its hind legs, and looked directly at Francis. Francis, filled with fear, froze in his tracks and shouldered his musket. The bear immediately dropped to all fours, let out a low growl, and charged toward Francis. Francis quickly aimed and shot the bear, killing it instantly and dropping it within a few feet of where he stood. With sweaty hands, Francis lowered his rifle and let out a slow breath.

Hearing the report from the musket, Richard, who had been dozing by the fire, grabbed his musket and jumped up, yelling as he ran toward the noise, "Are we being attacked? Francis, where are you?"

As he rushed to the front of the wagon, Richard tripped on a stump and fell head over heels to the ground.

Seeing Richard tumble, Francis fell to the ground and rolled around laughing uncontrollably. "Haha! It was just a bear, Richard! It was getting into our food box. But don't worry; it charged me, so I had to kill it!"

"Whew! I thought we were under attack!" Richard replied as he got up and brushed the dirt off his pants. "What is so funny?"

Still laughing on the ground, Francis said, "I've never seen you move that fast, Richard!"

Eliza, hearing the commotion and getting out of bed, approached and asked, "What is happening? I heard a gunshot and initially thought we were under attack. Then I heard laughter, so I came to see what was going on!"

"Richard thought we were under attack, but it was just a little 'ole bear. It was getting into our food supply, and it didn't like my interrupting its meal, so I had to kill it," Francis answered, grinning and looking at Richard.

"I heard the shot, then I tripped and fell while running to see what it was. Francis thought that was funny," Richard said. "I'm fine. Go back to bed."

"Thank goodness you're not hurt," Eliza replied. Then she added with a bit of sarcasm, "Please try to keep quiet — everyone's trying to sleep!"

"We will try," Richard said, grinning. "Good night, Eliza."

"Good night!" she replied, turning to go back to bed.

The next morning after breakfast, as the women cleaned up and packed the wagons, Francis and Richard skinned and butchered the bear, then packed the meat in a large box. They would have plenty to eat for the next day or two.

For the next two weeks, the group traveled through the Shenandoah Valley and southern Virginia, bordered by the Allegheny Mountains to the west and the Blue Ridge Mountains to the east. The road wound through rolling hills and valleys, surrounded by dense forests and vast grasslands. The smell of blooming rhododendrons and mountain laurels filled the air. Wildlife was abundant, so Francis and the others could easily get fresh meat.

Many small streams and creeks flowed through the valley, along with several rivers. When the group reached the James River, they were glad to find a ferry operated by Robert Looney. As expected, it took most of the day to ferry all the wagons across, so they set up camp after everyone had crossed.

While the woman unloaded food and cooking utensils from the wagons, Richard started a fire, and Francis and William hunted for game.

"Don't move, William," Francis said, raising his musket. "There's a big buck down in that draw."

"I see him. We need to get a little closer."

As the two slowly crept through the underbrush, the buck that had been feeding on some grass raised its head.

"Stop!" whispered Francis. "Just another twenty feet and we'll be close enough."

When the buck lowered its head again, the two kept stalking until they were within range. Francis raised his musket, took aim, fired, and the buck dropped right where it stood.

William exclaimed, "We'll eat well tonight!"

"That's for sure," Francis answered. "Let's gut it and haul it back to camp!"

When the two returned to camp, hauling the buck, Francis told Richard, "I shot him. Now you get to do the butchering!"

"I can do that," Richard replied, "but I get my pick of the best cuts of meat."

"Deal!" Francis replied.

The group feasted on venison backstrap and tenderloin that night. After supper, they all sat around the campfire until it burned down to embers.

"Time to turn in," Richard said, yawning. "We still have a long way to go, so we'll need to get an early start tomorrow."

"Good night, Francis," Anna said, smiling as their eyes met and she brushed her hand against his while heading to bed.

"Good night, Anna. Sleep well," Francis replied as he watched her walk off into the darkness.

Late one afternoon, the group arrived at the Big Lick settlement along the Roanoke River in Virginia. The Great Wagon Road ran through the center of the settlement, which included several log homes, a general store, a church, a blacksmith shop, and a tavern. The group set up camp just outside the settlement for the night, and after supper, Francis and Richard headed to the tavern.

"Welcome to Big Lick. How may I serve you?" the bartender asked as Francis and Richard entered the tavern and approached the bar.

"Two beers, please, sir," Richard replied.

The bartender placed two tankards of beer on the bar. "Where are you gentlemen from, and where are you headed?"

Francis lifted his tankard and took a long sip. "We come from Lancaster, and we plan on settling in Anson County in the colony of North Carolina."

"You will have plenty of company," the bartender said. "A lot of folks coming through here are headed there."

"We know several people who have already settled there. They wrote to families back in Lancaster, saying the land there is affordable and highly fertile. The landscape features rolling hills and meadows, with abundant hardwood forests, and the climate is milder than in Lancaster," Richard said, sipping his beer.

"I have heard similar stories," the bartender replied. "How has your journey been so far?"

"So far, we have been lucky. We had to replace a wagon wheel on this side of the Susquehanna River. That set us back half a day. Other than that, the trip has been smooth," Richard said.

Looking at Richard, Francis grinned and added, "Except for having to kill a little 'ole bear one night!"

The bartender served another traveler and turned to wipe the bar. "You should be careful as you go further south. Some northbound travelers told me bandits robbed them south of here, and there are also Indian raiding parties along the road."

"We will certainly keep an eye out for bandits and Indians," Francis said as he finished his beer and set the tankard on the counter.

Laying a sixpence on the bar, Richard said, "Thank you, sir, for the beers and the information." Then, as he and Francis turned to leave, he said, "We need to pick up a few supplies at the store before heading back to camp."

The bartender picked up the sixpence and said, "Thank you for stopping by. I hope you have a safe trip to North Carolina."

The next morning, while everyone was preparing to leave, Eliza said to Anna, "The water barrel is getting low. Take these buckets down to the creek and bring back some water." She then turned to Francis and asked, "Would you please go with her? She doesn't need to be in the woods down by the creek alone, and she will need help bringing the buckets full of water back up the hill."

"Yes, ma'am," Francis replied. Then, looking at Anna, he said, "Grab a bucket, Anna."

Anna smiled, grabbed a bucket, and they headed down the hill to the creek. About halfway there, because of the thick undergrowth,

Anna tripped and fell head over heels, causing her bucket to fly out of her hands.

"Oh, no! Are you hurt?" Francis asked as he set down his bucket and leaned over her.

"I'm fine, just a little embarrassed," she said, sitting up in a patch of running cedar.

"Let me help you up," Francis said as he took her hand.

As he lifted her off the ground, she lost her balance on the steep slope and fell into his arms. With their faces only inches apart, their eyes met, and she quickly kissed him.

"Oh, please forgive me, Francis! That was not proper! I shouldn't have done that, but I couldn't help myself!"

Startled, he looked at her and smiled, surprised and unsure how to respond, but glad it had happened.

He laughed and said, "No need to apologize, Anna. I enjoyed that!"

Then, still holding her, he continued, "I have noticed you stealing glances and smiling at me, so I wondered if you have feelings for me."

Anna, feeling embarrassed, admitted, "I do. You have no idea how many times I've dreamed of being held in your arms! I guess I'm just being silly."

Francis hesitated before he said, "No, you're not being silly. I have thought a lot about holding you in my arms, too."

For a moment, the two remained in each other's embrace, heads resting on shoulders, savoring the quiet of the morning and reflecting on what had been said.

Finally, Francis said, "I'm glad you kissed me, Anna. And I'm glad we shared how we feel."

"Me too, and I'm glad I no longer have to wonder how you feel about me."

Francis, suddenly recalling why they were there, released her and picked up his bucket. "This is nice, but we need to get water and head back. Everyone will want to know what took so long!"

Brushing some leaves and twigs off her skirt and picking up her bucket, Anna said, "No, we wouldn't want them to be suspicious, but you can get water with me anytime!"

The two continued toward the creek, filled their buckets, and then climbed back up the hill to the wagons. When they returned, the group was almost ready to leave, and nobody seemed concerned. After they dumped the water into the barrel, Anna climbed into her spot in the wagon, unable to contain her excitement, and Francis couldn't stop thinking about Anna and that first kiss.

Later that day, they crossed the Roanoke River without incident. The road south of the river was quite steep, so everyone had to get out of the wagons and help push. By nightfall, everyone was worn out and happy that it was finally time to rest. Francis shot and butchered a deer while the other men and women set up camp, gathered firewood, and started a fire.

After a supper of venison stew, and after the dishes were clean, everyone sat by the campfire, exhausted but enjoying the warmth of the fire on the cool evening.

When everyone began heading to bed, Anna stood and said, "Good night, everyone." Then she whispered, "Good night, Francis," as she brushed her hand against his cheek while no one was watching.

"Good night, Anna. Sleep well," Francis replied, watching her glance over her shoulder and smile as she walked away.

. After everyone went to bed, Francis, Richard, and William sat around the campfire talking about the information the bartender had given them when a sudden war cry from raiding warriors broke the silence. Arrows whistled through the air, piercing wagons and tearing through the canvas.

Francis, sitting on a log by the fire, shouted, "We are under attack!" then jumped up, grabbed his musket, and fired at the attackers while running for cover under a wagon.

Richard sprang up, musket in hand. He fired at the attackers, reloaded, and fired again before diving under a wagon.

As Francis reloaded, he heard screams coming from a nearby wagon. One warrior had climbed into the wagon, seized Hannah, the Brandons' youngest daughter, and was carrying her away.

"They've got Hannah!" Francis yelled at Richard as he started running toward the screams. "I'm going after her. Keep firing!"

As Hannah was being carried away, kicking and screaming, by the warrior, Francis chased after them while the other men continued firing at the attackers. He caught up with Hannah and her captor, grabbing the warrior by the shoulders. The warrior dropped Hannah to focus on this new threat. He withdrew a knife and faced Francis, anger flashing in his eyes. When the warrior swung the knife at Francis, Francis sidestepped and disarmed him, grabbing him by the neck and throwing him to the ground. After several minutes of wrestling and fighting on the dirt, the warrior struggled to his feet and ran off into the forest. Francis, hot, sweaty, and muddy from the struggle, cradled the terrified girl and carried her back to camp.

The skirmish was short but fierce. When the attackers finally retreated, two travelers from a different family had been killed, and several wagons bore the signs of battle.

"Anna, are you alright?" Francis asked as he looked into the back of the wagon where she was lying on her bed. "It was an Indian attack."

"Yes, I'm fine," Anna replied, sitting up. "I heard shouting and gunfire. I was *so* frightened, I didn't know what to do but hide under the covers!"

"Thank goodness! I was worried you might be hurt. There were a lot of arrows flying."

"No, just scared. What about you? Your clothes are muddy, and you look like you've been in a fight. Are you hurt?"

"No, I'm not injured. I had to fight off an Indian warrior trying to take Hannah, but I managed to save her. We fought them off, and they're gone now."

"Good! Thank you for checking on me, Francis. I'm so relieved neither of us is injured!" she said.

With heavy hearts and tearful eyes, graves were dug, the dead were laid to rest, and a brief funeral service was held. Realizing that staying would increase the risk of another attack, the group left at dawn the next day to continue their journey.

As the exhausted group entered North Carolina, the thick forests offered ideal concealment for threats.

"Keep a sharp eye out," Richard warned as he guided his wagon across a shallow creek. "There's no telling what or who might be hiding in this thick underbrush."

"We are ready for anything," Francis answered, taking his musket off his shoulder and holding it in a ready position.

As Richard urged the oxen up the opposite bank of the creek, two armed bandits stepped out from the underbrush and blocked the path in front of Richard's wagon with their pistols raised and faces covered by scarves.

"Get down from your wagons and empty your pockets," the leader ordered, pointing his pistol at Richard.

As Richard wrapped the reins around the brake handle and stood up, Francis, standing in the creek behind the wagon, stepped out and shouldered his musket. "Drop your pistols and put your hands up!"

Startled, the bandit leader aimed his pistol at Francis, who immediately fired, hitting the bandit in the shoulder.

"Damn!" the bandit shouted as he dropped his pistol and fell to his knees.

Richard immediately drew his pistol and aimed it at the other bandit. Knowing they were outmatched, the bandit turned and ran back into the bushes.

The leader, clutching his shoulder, stood up and hobbled into the woods while shouting obscenities.

"Good work, Francis," Richard said as he sat back down and took hold of the reins.

"They will not bother us again," Francis replied as he walked up the creek bank, picked up the pistol the bandit had dropped, and stood by the wagon.

"I guess not," said Richard. "But let's not tempt fate. Let's move on."

◆◆◆

By early November, the group reached the Yadkin River. The water level was high, and the current was strong—a possibility they had discussed earlier in their journey.

"Everyone except the drivers out of the wagons, please," Francis said, standing on the bank of the swollen river.

The women and children jumped down from the wagons, leaving only the drivers to steer their wagons through the swollen river. After the first two wagons crossed safely, George started across in his wagon.

Richard yelled, "Keep moving, or you will get mired down in the muddy bottom," as he watched George maneuver his wagon in the middle of the river, where the fast-moving current swirled above the wheel hubs. One wheel sank into a hole in the muddy riverbed, causing the wagon to tilt and nearly tip over. Before George could urge the oxen forward to correct the problem in the strong current, the wagon was almost swept away. George urged the oxen forward, righting the wagon, but part of its valuable cargo spilled out and was lost to the depths.

Having already crossed to the other side on his horse, Francis dropped his musket and guided the horse into the murky water. He retrieved most of the floating objects, but several heavier items sank into the depths.

After all the wagons had crossed, Richard and Francis tied a rope to trees on both sides of the river so the women and children could hold on as they waded hip-deep through the strong, cold current. Once across, the group camped for the night to rest, dry off, and let the items they had retrieved from the river dry.

"Meet me on the back side of the lead wagon tonight after everyone is in bed," Francis whispered in Anna's ear as he walked past her after supper.

When the campfire died down to embers and everyone was in bed, Francis, who was on watch by the fire, stood and walked behind the lead wagon to wait for Anna.

After waiting a while, Anna got out of bed and climbed down from the back of her wagon, thinking: *What could he want out here in the moonlight? Does he want to talk or ask me something? He knows how I feel about him, and he said he has feelings for me. Maybe he'll kiss me! I can't wait to be with him again!*

After what felt like forever to Francis, Anna walked up, her hair shining in the moonlight, and said, "Good evening, Francis! It's nice out tonight."

"It's a beautiful night. I didn't know if you would come," Francis said.

"I would never miss a chance to be with you," Anna replied tenderly, looking up at Francis.

He embraced her, and they stood close under the moonlight, with the calls of owls and whip-poor-wills in the distance. Holding her tightly and gazing into her eyes, he gently lifted her chin, and as their lips touched, he softly kissed her for a long moment.

When the kiss ended, she said, "Umm, that was *so* nice! I've been kissed once before, by a boy I knew in Lancaster. But not like that! I love you, Francis! I've known it for a while, but I was too afraid to tell you because I didn't know how you felt, until you shared your feelings at that creek."

"I love you too, Anna! I love the sparkle in your eyes and the smile on your tender lips when you look at me. I adore the sway in your walk and the way you carry yourself with such grace. I love how your hair shines in the moonlight and how you have such a gentle, caring spirit. And I truly love how it feels when you're in my arms and the way you kiss me so sweetly!"

They shared another long, lingering kiss, Anna melting in his arms, before Francis pulled away and said, "Anna, you should leave now before this goes any further. I don't want you to go, but we shouldn't be alone together any longer. And besides, there's always a chance someone might find us here."

"I know. I don't want to go either, but you're probably right." Anna said with regret. "Good night, Francis."

"Good night," Francis said, kissing her again before she slowly slipped out of his embrace and walked away.

Francis returned to the campfire to keep watch. He added a log, and as he watched it ignite, he sat down and thought about Anna for the rest of the evening. Anna slipped back into bed unnoticed and fell asleep thinking of Francis and that passionate kiss.

Since the Irish Settlement in Anson County was just ten miles away, they set out early the next morning, eager to complete their journey. The group arrived by mid-afternoon and was pleased to see smoke curling from chimneys, plowed fields, and sturdy houses and barns.

The settlement, though still new, was bustling with activity. Several merchants had set up stalls along the dirt streets, selling a variety of goods, including fresh produce, tools, cloth, hats, muskets, candles, and shoes. The sound of a blacksmith hammering tools and horseshoes echoed through the streets, and the smell of wood smoke and cooking meat filled the air. People greeted each other in front of the wooden church at the end of one street. A tavern stood in the center of town, with a simple sign out front advertising rooms and meals.

Eliza exhaled deeply as the tired travelers brought their wagons to a stop in front of the tavern. They had finally reached their destination. The Great Wagon Road had tested them but hadn't broken them. Ahead lay the tough work of claiming land, clearing it, and building homes, but for now, they would rest, thankful to have arrived safely.

7

A New Beginning in North Carolina

In 1748, the Irish Settlement was a small but thriving frontier community in western North Carolina, then part of Anson County.

The sun was just above the eastern horizon when Richard stepped out of the tavern where his family had settled for the night after spending months sleeping in the wagons or on the ground.

As he walked down the dirt street lined with shops and offices, a man approaching him called out, "Richard! What a surprise to see you here! How long has it been since we last met at the Hickory Tree Tavern in Lancaster?"

"Christiaan Janson! What an unexpected pleasure! That was more than a decade ago. So, you made it to North Carolina!" Richard said, nodding and tipping his hat.

"Yes, I did, and I have a farm about five miles from here," Christiaan replied. "When did you arrive?"

"We arrived yesterday and are staying temporarily at the tavern down the street."

"It is good to see you again!"

"And you, too," Richard replied.

"When I arrived here, I applied for and received a land grant from Lord Granville, and I cleared the land and built a house and a barn," Christiaan said. "You should apply for a grant as soon as possible before all the land is gone."

"Thank you for that advice. I will keep that in mind."

"I was allowed to construct a temporary cabin on the land before my grant was approved. Once it was approved, I built our permanent home. If you and your family need a place to stay until you secure your land, you are welcome to use that temporary cabin as long as necessary." He then added, "The cabin is small, but it will keep your family warm and dry until you can get land and build a home."

"Thank you, sir. You are very kind. I will take you up on that offer."

The November sky was cloudless and a beautiful light blue as Richard opened the door to the little cabin, startling a family of raccoons that had entered through a hole in the roof. They hissed and bared their teeth, but quickly exited through the hole.

The modest cabin was a simple log structure with a cedar-shake roof. It was set on the bank of a creek in the back of a large field surrounded by hardwood forests. A dirt path led to the Irish Settlement, about three miles away. There were three rooms in the cabin—a central living/cooking area in the front, and two large bedrooms in the rear. Except for a few rickety chairs scattered about, the cabin was empty. A fireplace was on the side wall, and a stack of firewood rested beside the hearth. The journey had been long, and although their new home was modest, it provided a sense of security they had lacked for far too long.

Eliza shook her head and sighed as she surveyed the three-room log cabin with its dirt floor. "It will have to do."

Francis stood just inside the doorway, brushing dust off his coat. "It will keep us warm and dry. Christiaan said we can stay as long as we need."

The family looked around, taking in the simplicity of their new home. It was a far cry from the comforts they were used to in Lancaster, but it was a start.

Richard nodded, resting his hands on his hips as he surveyed the space. "It's more than we could have asked for. We'll make do. Let's get everything inside and put away. We'll need to be up early tomorrow to prepare for the winter. There's work to be done."

The group fell into a comfortable rhythm, unloading the furniture and other items they had brought from Lancaster and organizing their belongings inside the cabin. Although still weary from the journey, they were determined to make the little cabin feel like home.

As the family settled into the cramped temporary cabin, Francis busied himself with building and lighting a fire in the fireplace. Meanwhile, Eliza and Anna sewed sheets together to make mattresses, and Francis and William filled them with straw from the field while Richard and Francis patched the hole in the roof. While the cabin provided shelter, it had drafty walls and a leaky roof during heavy rains. Despite these challenges, the family's determination remained firm.

Days flew by as they tended to chores like caring for livestock, gathering firewood, and settling into their temporary home. Richard sold the wagons and oxen, using the money to buy bed frames, a few more chairs, a table, and other household items. James and Francis hunted for game to supplement their modest supplies, while Eliza cooked and cleaned the cabin, and Anna took care of the younger children.

As he ate breakfast one morning, Richard looked up from his plate. "Eliza, we need to have our own land and a proper house. I'm going to the settlement today to apply for a land grant."

Eliza nodded; her eyes sparkled with hope. "I agree. This place is small. We need land and a home we can call our own."

After breakfast, Richard rode into the Irish Settlement and stopped his horse in front of a modest wooden building with a simple sign outside that read: 'Land Office'. Dismounting, he dusted off his coat and stepped inside. The dimly lit interior smelled of damp wood and ink. Sitting behind a cluttered, dilapidated oak desk was an older clerk with thinning gray hair and spectacles on the bridge of his nose.

Tipping his head down and looking over the spectacles, he greeted Richard. "Good day, sir."

Richard removed his hat and stepped up to the desk. "And to you as well. My name is Richard Brandon. I've come to inquire about acquiring land. I was told I could apply for a grant from Lord Granville."

The clerk nodded. "Aye, that is correct. I am Thomas Child, Lord Granville's land agent for Anson County. Lord Granville grants land to settlers willing to improve it. Do you have a parcel of land in mind?"

His tone was businesslike, but a hint of curiosity lingered as he awaited Richard's response.

Richard nodded. "I've seen land between here and the Yadkin River. Fertile soil, good for farming. I would like to settle there with my family."

"Most of those tracts are taken. There is good land west of here, near Buffalo Creek. Rolling hills with a combination of meadows and woodlands."

"That sounds good," Richard replied. "How do I apply?"

As Mr. Child shuffled through a stack of documents, finally retrieving a form, he explained the process. "You must fill out this form to apply for a grant. There's a fee, of course, and a requirement to cultivate the land within a set number of years."

Richard placed his hands on the desk. "I understand. What size tract can a man apply for?"

"Most grants range from 100 to 640 acres, depending on the petitioner's ability to settle and improve the land. Are you prepared to work the land?"

Richard straightened. "Aye. My family and I aim to farm, raise livestock, and establish homesteads. I have three sons and four stepsons, and all are strong and willing to work the land."

Mr. Child nodded approvingly. "Then you'll do well. Look at this map showing available tracts, then fill out this petition stating the tract number, acreage, and intended use. The surveyor will mark the boundaries. If everything is in order, I will approve it."

Richard glanced at the map, then dipped his quill in ink and meticulously completed the form, signing his name. "How long will approval take?"

"It may take several weeks or longer, depending on the surveyor's schedule. Once the survey has been completed and I have approved it, the land is yours—provided you fulfill the settlement conditions."

Richard handed back the completed form. "That sounds good."

The clerk smiled, reviewed the form, and signed his name on the document. "Indeed, Mr. Brandon. If all goes well, you'll soon be the rightful owner of a fine stretch of Carolina soil. Check back with me in a few weeks to see if you've been approved."

Richard nodded, walked to the door, and replaced his hat before stepping out into the sun. A hopeful future lay before him on the fertile frontier of North Carolina.

Later that month, while he was in town, Richard stopped by the Land Office to check the status of his land grant application.

"Good day to you, Mr. Brandon," the clerk greeted, eyeing Richard as he stepped inside.

"And to you as well, Mr. Child," Richard replied, removing his hat and approaching the desk. "I'm here to inquire whether my grant application has been approved."

Shuffling some papers on his desk and picking one up, Mr. Childs replied, "Yes, you've been approved, sir. You are now the proud owner of six hundred and forty acres along Buffalo Creek, about six miles west of here. All that's left is to sign a few documents, and the land is yours."

"That's wonderful news!" Richard said, reaching for the quill and dipping it into the inkwell.

Mr. Child dipped his quill into the inkpot and scratched a few lines onto the document before sliding it across the desk. "Here's your official grant. Sign here."

Richard carefully inscribed his name on the document, sealing his claim to the land. Mr. Child studied the signature and then gave a nod of satisfaction. "Everything's in order. You'll need to get this recorded at the courthouse, but as of today, the land is yours; six hundred and forty acres of prime ground along Buffalo Creek. Good land for farming, I'd say."

Richard let out a slow breath. "I reckon it is," he said, tucking the parchment safely inside his coat. "And I intend to make good use of it."

Mr. Child offered a knowing smile. "Then I wish you good fortune, Mr. Brandon. May your home stand strong and your crops be plentiful." Then, remembering Richard's previous inquiry, he added, "When you applied for this land on Buffalo Creek, you inquired about land near the Yadkin River. There was no land available near the Yadkin then, but a tract has since become available. If you are still interested, you can apply for it."

Richard's eyes lit up. "Absolutely."

"You'll just need to fill out another application and pay the application fee," Mr. Child said, handing him the form.

By the time Richard set down his quill, he wasn't just the owner of six hundred and forty acres along Buffalo Creek; he had also applied for another six hundred and forty acres along the Yadkin River. Before replacing his hat and heading for the door, he lingered a moment, gazing at the paper in his hand. Then, with a deep breath, he stepped outside into the bright North Carolina sun, ready to begin his new life on Buffalo Creek.

When Francis, Richard, and his two adult sons, James and William, arrived at the land they could now call home, the morning sun had just peeked over the horizon. The forest was thick with towering oaks and hickories, their canopies casting long shadows on the ground below.

"This is fine land," Richard said, resting his hands on his hips as he surveyed the landscape. "Rich soil, fresh water from the creek, and plenty of timber."

"Aye, Father," William agreed, brushing a hand across his forehead. "We'll have to work fast before the weather turns. We'll need shelter before the first frost."

Francis grinned. "I'm glad we helped the Thompsons build their house last month. We know what to do."

Richard nodded. "Then let's get to it."

For the homesite, Richard had chosen a flat spot on a gentle rise in a large meadow bordered by hardwood and pine forests on three sides and Buffalo Creek on the fourth.

"This will be the perfect spot," Richard said, surveying the area. "Flat, high ground, tall, straight pine trees to cut logs for the walls, and plenty of water in the creek, just a hundred yards away."

He took up his axe and swung it at the base of a pine tree, the sound of wood cracking filling the air. James and Francis followed suit, and soon the men had felled several trees, cut off the limbs, and trimmed them to size. They hitched a horse and hauled the logs to the homesite clearing. After several days, they had laid the foundation with notched logs stacked and interlocked at the corners. Then, after many weeks, the rough walls of the cabin rose, sturdy and sure. The air was thick with the scent of fresh-cut wood and sweat.

One day, as the four men took a break for a meal of salted pork and cornbread, Francis glanced up at the gathering clouds and wiped his hands on his trousers. "What about the roof? We'll need shingles."

Richard smiled. "We'll split some wooden shakes from a cedar tree tomorrow. In the meantime, we'll make a temporary roof with branches and bark to keep out the rain."

James leaned against a felled log, looking toward the mostly finished cabin. "What about a floor?"

"Brother Matias mentioned on our trip here that the Moravians have a sawmill. We can get floorboards there," Francis replied.

"Great idea!" Richard said.

"They also produce shingles. We can take the wagon to Bethabara and pick up the shingles and enough lumber for a floor," Francis said, eyeing the cabin.

Richard nodded with satisfaction in his eyes. "Aye. A strong home built with our own hands. A place for our family to grow."

With renewed determination, they returned to work. After several months of laboring from sunrise to sunset, the men completed the house. It featured a pine floor and a cedar-shake roof. It included a spacious living area, a kitchen, four roomy bedrooms on the ground level, and a large loft area for storage and additional sleeping space. They collected stones from the creek to build two fireplaces, one in the living area and another in the kitchen for cooking.

As Richard ushered Eliza into their new home, she exclaimed, "Oh, Richard! This is wonderful! You men have outdone expectations!" Of course, her first stop was the kitchen, where she immediately began planning the locations of the kitchen table, chairs, and cupboards for storing dishes, utensils, and food. By the end of the week, the family had moved their modest belongings from the temporary cabin to their new home.

After several more months, the men finished building a barn with four horse stalls and a hayloft above, along with a chicken coop and fencing for a pasture beside the creek. They settled the horses into their stalls, while Francis herded some cows that Richard had bought into the pasture, and housed several chickens and a rooster he had purchased in the chicken coop.

In 1753, Rowan County was formed from Anson County, and the Irish Settlement was renamed Rowan Courthouse. The Moravian town of Salem became the primary trade center within the Wachovia settlement.

By late spring, Richard and Eliza Brandon, along with their children and stepchildren, had comfortably settled into their new home near Buffalo Creek. Richard also owned six hundred forty acres along the Yadkin River and had purchased another 640 acres near Grant's Creek.

Living in the same house was challenging for Francis and Anna because of their feelings for each other. When they thought no one was watching, they would look at each other with knowing smiles, and sometimes, when they were alone, they would hold hands.

One evening after supper, as daylight was fading, Francis took Anna by the hand, and they quietly slipped out of the house and walked to the barn. Walking behind the barn, out of sight of the house, they stood close together and embraced as the moon rose over the horizon. Francis looked into her eyes and pulled her closer. Then, as he gently swept strands of hair away from her face, their lips finally met. Time stood still as his gentle kiss lingered, warm and firm against her open lips, his muscular arms holding her tightly, his warm body against hers, and their hearts beating together.

When the kiss ended, she said, "Umm, that was *so* nice! I love you, Francis!"

"I love you too, Anna! I adore your tender lips and the way you melt in my arms when we kiss. I love how your hair shimmers in the moonlight. And I love how it feels when you're in my arms!"

"And I love it when you hold me tight in your strong arms!

They shared another long, lingering kiss, Anna melting in his arms, before Francis pulled away and said, "We should go back to the house before this goes any further. I don't want to, but we shouldn't be alone together any longer. And besides, there's always a chance someone might find us here."

"I know. I don't want to go either, but you're probably right." Anna said with regret.

After one more lingering kiss, they slowly returned to the house. Anna slipped into bed and fell asleep, thinking about Francis and those passionate kisses. The stairs creaked softly as Francis climbed them, and as he lay in bed, he couldn't stop thinking of Anna.

The next day, as Anna sat by the fireplace knitting, Francis came in and said, "Come and walk with me, Anna. I need to ask you something."

Anna, curious, set her knitting down, and the two of them headed out toward the barn.

As they sat on the pasture fence, they held hands, and Francis said, "Anna, we've had feelings for each other for some time now. I still cherish the memory of that time so long ago when we went to get water at the creek, and you surprised me with a quick kiss. Then, last night, when we were alone in the moonlight, we held each other close, shared several long kisses, and confessed our love for each other."

Francis took a breath and looked into her eyes. "Anna, I love you, and I want to spend the rest of my life with you. Will you marry me?"

"Oh, Francis! I love you too, and I cannot imagine life without you! I would be so happy to be your wife! Yes! I will marry you!"

Francis was so happy that he lost his balance and almost fell off the fence as Anna giggled.

"Thank you!" he said. "I promise I will love and care for you as long as I live. I will ask Richard for his blessing at the first opportunity!"

8
Life in Rowan County

The leaves of the trees above them swayed in the gentle breeze as Francis and Richard split logs at the edge of the woods one afternoon in May. Francis stopped, wiped the sweat from his brow, and glanced at Richard, who was picking up another log.

Francis cleared his throat and said, "Richard."

"What, Francis?"

Francis's mind was filled with doubt as he worried about what he was about to ask Richard. *Is this the right time to bring this up? What if he says 'No'? Maybe I should wait for a better time? Why is this so hard? I'm a grown man!*

Francis set his axe aside and took a deep breath. "There's something I've been meaning to talk to you about."

Richard didn't look up right away. Swinging his axe again, he split a thick log down the center, straightened, and turned to Francis.

"What?" he asked, his voice calm but curious.

Francis nodded. "It's about Anna."

Richard's expression didn't change, but Francis could tell he had his full attention now as Richard leaned on his axe handle and looked directly at him. "What about her?"

Francis took another deep breath and exhaled slowly. "I have asked for her hand in marriage, and she said 'Yes.' I would like your blessing."

For a moment, the only sounds were the rustling of leaves and the chirping of birds. Richard studied Francis for a moment. He had noticed how Francis looked at Anna, and how she looked at him. He had some suspicions when they were traveling on the Great Wagon Road, but he had brushed them off. Recently, he had seen them sitting together on the pasture fence, hand in hand, and he knew this moment was coming.

Francis's mind raced as he waited for what seemed like an eternity for Richard's reply. *Alright. I've asked him. What will he say? If he says "No," what will I do, and what will Anna say?*

"Do you love her?" Richard finally asked.

"Yes, sir. With all my heart," Francis replied earnestly. "And she loves me. I'll do right by her. I'll work hard, provide for her, and take care of her always."

Richard exhaled, looking off toward the trees for a long moment. Again, it seemed like an eternity to Francis.

Then he looked back at Francis. "You're a good man, Francis. Hardworking, honest."

He's going to say "No," Francis thought.

Richard continued, "And I've seen how Anna lights up when you come around."

He studied Francis for another long moment, then let out a breath and nodded slowly. "Then you have my blessing."

A huge smile broke across Francis's face. "Thank you, Richard. That means everything to me."

Richard gave a small grunt, then picked up another log, setting it onto the splitting stump.

Francis grabbed a log and turned back to Richard. "When Anna and I marry, we'll need a place to begin our life together—a home where we can raise a family. Would you consider selling me the tract of land you own bordering Grant's Creek?"

Richard nodded thoughtfully. "That's a fine piece of land—640 acres—but I have no use for it. I already have more than I'll ever need," Richard paused momentarily as their eyes met. "So yes, as a wedding gift, I'll sell it to you at a very fair price."

A grin spread across Francis's face. "Thank you, Richard!"

Francis picked up his axe once more, and the two men resumed their work.

After he purchased the land from Richard, Francis immediately started building his new home with the help of his brothers, brothers-in-law, and Richard.

The two-story house was located off the main road leading to the Irish Settlement, at the back of a ten-acre field of broom straw bordered by hardwood forests. The post-and-beam construction featured weatherboard siding and a gable roof covered with cedar shakes. A covered porch ran the entire length of the front.

Inside, a central hallway extended from the front door to the back door, with a staircase beside it leading upstairs. Two large rooms, situated on either side of the hallway, provided ample space for living and entertaining. The room at the back, on the left, was a dining room, while the one at the rear, on the right, served as a library and office. The two front rooms were sitting rooms, each with framed windows on the exterior walls, along with a large fireplace and hearth for heat. Wide hand-hewn pine boards covered the floors, nailed to the joists with cut nails.

There were four spacious bedrooms upstairs off a central hallway. Each bedroom had a fireplace connected to the chimneys from the lower fireplaces for heating.

All the interior walls were covered with lath, finished with plaster, and painted. The downstairs rooms also featured raised paneling, wainscoting, and chair-rail molding.

The kitchen was a separate building at the back of the main house. It featured a large room with a big fireplace and hearth used for cooking and food preparation, along with two smaller rooms—one for storing food and the other for dishes and utensils. That room also had a tub for washing dishes with hot water and homemade lye soap.

◆ ◆ ◆

In September, Anna entered the room where Eliza was sitting by the hearth, mending a pair of trousers.

"Come in, Anna," Eliza said, motioning to the seat beside her. "We need to finalize the wedding plans."

Anna smoothed her apron and sat down, folding her hands in her lap. "Yes, ma'am. I am eager to know what else must be done."

Eliza gave a nod of approval. "Francis and the men have finished the new house and have started on the barn."

"I know. I was out there yesterday. The house is amazing!" Anna said as she smiled. "I will do my best to be a good wife to him."

"I know you will," Eliza said, patting Anna's hand. "Now, there are matters to attend to. We've only got a few weeks. Have you finished your gown?"

Anna hesitated. "I have been sewing it by candlelight, but I still have the hem to finish."

"We shall work on it together," Eliza said firmly. "And your veil—white, as befits a woman entering marriage in purity."

"Yes, ma'am," Anna agreed. "And will you still bake the wedding bread for the party after the wedding?"

"Yes, I will, and the neighbors have offered to bring a ham, potato salad, cider, and plenty of corn and beans from this season's harvest. It will be a grand celebration!"

Anna glanced toward the window, where the sun was setting over the fields. "I pray all goes well."

Eliza squeezed her hand. "It will, Anna. You and Francis are meant for each other. I've seen the way he looks at you, and how you look at him. Now, let's finish that hem."

As the wedding day dawned, the sky was clear and the sun shone brightly; the leaves were at their peak, displaying a full range of fall colors. The venue was Thyatira Presbyterian Church, a modest wood-frame building in Rowan County, a few miles from Francis's land. The minister, dressed in a dark robe with a white stole, stood at the front, his Bible open, waiting for the bride. At the altar, Francis straightened his coat, his face glowing with anticipation.

Anna ascended the front steps of the church, her simple linen gown clean and pressed, her white headdress sitting neatly over her braided hair, with a veil covering her face. Next to her, Richard walked with solemn pride. As they entered the church from the rear, the congregation stood, and the bride and her father slowly made their way up the aisle toward the altar. As the congregation took their seats, the minister spoke the familiar opening words: "Dearly beloved, we are gathered here in the sight of God…"

The vows were spoken in steady voices. Francis took Anna's hand, sliding a simple silver band onto her finger. When the blessing was given and the couple was pronounced husband and wife, a cheer and applause erupted, and after Francis gently kissed his bride, the couple walked down the aisle arm in arm, grinning from ear to ear.

Outside on the church grounds, friends and family had set up tables, where a feast of ham, potato salad, corn, beans, cider, and the wedding bread made by Eliza awaited. The guests danced to the sound of a fiddle, congratulated the new couple, feasted, and enjoyed each other's company. Francis and Anna stood together, holding each other close and enjoying the warm afternoon sun.

As the sun set below the horizon, the guests threw rice at the new couple as they boarded a buggy and headed to their new home, their future together just starting.

By 1755, Francis and Anna had been married for two years and had a one-year-old named Rebecca. The town of Rowan Courthouse was renamed Salisbury, becoming the county seat of Rowan County. To commemorate Salisbury's designation as the county seat, the town hosted a grand celebration attended by many, including most of the Brandons and Lockes. Eliza was babysitting Rebecca, so it was already dark by the time Francis and Anna retrieved their daughter and returned home from the festivities.

As they were getting ready for bed, Anna, unable to contain her excitement, exclaimed, "Francis, I have some wonderful news!"

"What is it?" Francis asked as he turned the bedcovers down.

"I'm with child!" Anna replied, her face beaming.

Francis paused momentarily as he looked into Anna's glowing eyes. "That's fantastic news! How far along are you?"

"About two months, as far as I can tell," Anna replied as she settled into her side of the bed and started feeding Rebecca.

"Have you told my mother yet?" Francis asked, slipping into bed himself.

"No, silly! I wanted you to be the first to know! I'll tell her and my father tomorrow."

"Oh, I am so excited! I'm going to be a father again!" Francis said as he cuddled up to Anna, stroked her hair, and kissed her gently. "So, when are you due?"

"Around the end of the year. I hope it's a boy! Rebecca needs a little brother! I cannot wait to tell Father and Eliza!"

After finishing feeding Rebecca and settling her for the night, Francis and Anna blew out the candles and cuddled under the covers, excited about the new addition to their family.

The next day, Anna visited her stepmother, Eliza. When she entered the house, Eliza was sitting at the kitchen table, peeling apples.

Anna pulled up a chair beside her stepmother. "I have some wonderful news—I'm going to have another baby!"

Eliza, grinning, put down the knife and wiped her hands on her apron. "Oh, that is *wonderful* news, Anna! When are you due?"

"Probably late in the year. I'm about two months along now."

"Just in time for Christmas, maybe?"

"Yes, hopefully by Christmas. That will be something extra to celebrate! Where is Father?"

"He and Matthew are planting the tract down by the creek."

"Please do not tell him! I want to be the one to share the good news with him."

Agreed. I won't. I'll let you tell him the good news.

One morning in late December, as Francis walked into the living room, Anna was standing beside a chair near the fireplace, her midsection clenched. "Francis, it's time. Go fetch Eliza. Tell her to come quickly!"

"Go upstairs and get into bed. I'll be back as soon as I can," Francis said as he headed out the back door.

He ran to the barn, saddled a horse, and galloped to Eliza's house, about five miles away. When Francis returned, Eliza was close behind on her horse.

As Eliza entered the home and ran up to the bedroom, Anna was lying in bed, moaning.

"Francis, go boil some water and get some clean towels," Eliza ordered. "The baby's almost ready to come."

By noon, Francis and Anna were the proud new parents of a baby boy. They named him John after Francis's father. This latest arrival gave the family something special to celebrate for Christmas that year.

However, the celebrations were short-lived. A few months later, in the spring of 1756, tragedy struck. Anna's father, Richard Brandon, aged 65, passed away peacefully after a brief illness.

The morning was cloudy and cool as the funeral procession moved from inside Thyatira Presbyterian Church to the cemetery behind it. Francis stood beside the grave, his hat gripped in his hands, his head bowed. A simple pine coffin lay next to the open grave. Anna and Eliza, with dark shawls draped over their shoulders, stood beside Francis. Huddled together were the other Brandon and Locke children, heads bowed and tears in their eyes. As the minister recited a solemn prayer, Anna's mind drifted back to when her father was full of life: his laughter echoing across the fields, his reassuring voice at home, his drive, and his kindness. As the preacher finished delivering the eulogy and the coffin was lowered into the ground, the mourners slowly drifted away, offering words of condolence before departing down the dirt path.

When they were alone, Francis exhaled with a look of sorrow in his eyes. Anna stared at the simple casket resting in the grave. "It doesn't feel real, Francis. He was sitting at our table just last week, talking with you and the boys about the upcoming planting season."

Francis nodded. "Yes, and now he's gone. I will miss hearing his voice greet me when I enter his house. Richard was like a father to me."

"He was a good, kind man and full of life. I know he would not want us to be sad," Eliza offered.

"I know, but I will miss him," Francis replied.

Anna gently cradled his arm. "I know, Francis. I will miss him, too."

Francis took a deep breath, and with his arm around Anna, the three slowly walked home.

9

The Locke Brothers in Business

The trade in deerskins and other goods was a vital part of the colonial economy in the 18th century. European settlers and Native American tribes engaged in a mutually beneficial relationship: Native Americans supplied deerskins, which were in high demand in Europe for making leather goods, while Europeans provided manufactured items such as weapons, tools, and textiles. Charles Town served as a key port for exporting deerskins to Great Britain.

One morning in late spring of 1756, Francis was at Murdoch's Hardware Store in Salisbury buying seed corn for planting. He was standing at the counter when a young man entered the store carrying an armful of animal pelts.

"Good morning, sir. You have some fine-looking skins there," Francis said, eyeing the armload of skins.

"Yes, sir. I tanned these hides last month. I'm here to trade them in."

"My name is Francis Locke. Whom do I have the pleasure of addressing?"

"My name is Daniel Boone. I live with my new bride along the Yadkin River east of here."

"Boone? Are you kin to Squire Boone?"

"Yes, sir. That's my father."

"I am acquainted with your father. He's the justice of the peace here in Rowan County. He's a fine man."

"Thank you, sir. I will tell him I met you."

"What can you get for these skins?" Francis asked.

Daniel laid the pelts on the counter. "I can get a dollar for a good doeskin. Or a small hatchet, or about 60 musket balls. For ten buckskin pelts, I can get a long rifle. These beaver pelts can bring up to ten shillings each. They make beaver-skin hats with them."

"You're a very industrious young man. It is a pleasure to meet you, Daniel, and I wish you well."

"And it is a pleasure to meet you, sir," Daniel replied.

Later that afternoon, Francis rode his horse along the dirt path toward his brother Matthew's homestead, the scent of smoke from the cabin's chimney filling the air. When he reached the clearing, his younger brother, Matthew, was stacking firewood beside the house.

Matthew glanced up and wiped his brow as Francis dismounted. "Hello, Francis. What brings you here this late in the day?"

Francis jumped down from his horse. "I was in Salisbury earlier today. I met a man at Murdoch's who started me thinking."

"About what?"

Francis stepped closer, lowering his voice. "There is a genuine opportunity in trade. And I reckon we ought to be the ones to seize it."

Matthew placed the last log on the pile and brushed sawdust off his hands. "Trade? What kind of trade?"

"Transport. Moving goods among the Catawba and Saponi Indians, Salisbury, Charles Town, and the Moravian settlement at Salem. Currently, there's very little organized transport. The Indians have goods to trade—furs, deerskins, beaver pelts, and herbs—and they need supplies from the settlements. Charles Town has manufactured goods from Europe. The Moravians produce furniture, pottery, and tools. They also operate a sawmill where they produce lumber and other construction materials, and they brew beer and distill whiskey. Salisbury is growing every day. I believe we can earn a good living transporting goods between these locations and either selling or trading them."

Matthew exhaled, rubbing his chin. "Sounds like a grand idea, Francis, but how will we manage it? We are just two men with a wagon and a few horses."

"Aye, but that is where we start," Francis said, his eyes shining enthusiastically. "We run a few trips, prove ourselves reliable, and reinvest in wagons, more stock, and maybe even hire a hand or two."

"While at Murdoch's, I met a young man named Daniel Boone. His father is Squire Boone, the justice of the peace for Rowan County. Daniel is a hunter and trapper, and he was there trading animal pelts—deer and beaver—for goods. A fine doeskin can fetch a dollar or a hatchet, and ten buckskins can be exchanged for a long rifle."

Matthew stroked his chin as he considered the proposition. "The road to Charles Town is long and dangerous, Francis. Bandits roam those roads, and storms can wash them out overnight. And what about the Catawba Indians? They ain't always eager to trust settlers."

Francis nodded. "That is why we take our time and build relationships. I will speak with Red Hawk at the Catawba camp tomorrow. I know his people need muskets, powder, and tools. They can provide deerskins. We bring them what they need, trade fair, and earn their trust.

"As for the dangers on the road, we'll travel smart, learn the land well, and arm ourselves properly."

"There are bandits on the road to Charles Town. And roaming Indians."

"We confronted bandits and Indians before on the trip here from Lancaster. We will arm ourselves so that no bandits dare to rob us. And we can negotiate with any Indians we encounter."

Matthew sighed, then asked, "So, where do we start?"

Francis grinned. "We start with a trip to Charles Town with deerskins from the Catawba Indians to trade for English-made goods; then we take those to the Moravians in Salem and trade for furniture and good tools—hatchets, knives, even farming implements—which we can sell in Salisbury. If we do it right, we'll have enough profit to plan our next run to Charles Town."

Matthew shook his head. "Aye, brother. I'm in. Let's see if we can turn your idea into something real."

Francis clasped his brother's hand firmly. "You will not regret it, Matthew. We are going to build something worthwhile—just you wait."

The two brothers stood together as the last light of day faded into twilight, planning their new adventure. They discussed the best routes, supplies, and the potential challenges and dangers, their voices filled with anticipation and determination.

◆◆◆

The next day, Francis rode to the Catawba camp near the Yadkin River. Women and children rushed to greet him, and several dogs ran up and barked as he rode his horse into the camp.

A Native American man dressed in a deerskin loincloth and moccasins, with a single feather in his black hair that rested on his shoulders, met him as he dismounted. He wore body paint and silver bracelets on his tattooed upper arms, and he had a knife tucked in a deerskin sheath between the loincloth and his olive skin.

Francis bowed. "My name is Francis Locke. I am here to talk to you about a trade."

The man, obviously a ranking member of the Catawba tribe, raised his hand and said, "I Red Hawk. What you trade?"

"I need deerskins. In exchange, I can offer muskets, powder, knives, hatchets, and bright cloth.

"We need those. How many deerskins?"

"As many as you can provide."

"When?"

"By early summer."

"I can have many deerskins by the strawberry moon."

"That would be good. I will come back then," Francis replied, raising his hand in a sign of peace and turning to mount his horse.

In early summer, Francis returned to the Catawba camp with his wagon. As he jumped down from the wagon, Red Hawk greeted him, standing beside a pile of deerskins outside a round, bark-covered hut.

"Red Hawk, it is good to see you again. The hunting must have been good. These deerskins are of fine quality," Francis said, bowing slightly and picking up a skin.

"Hunting good. Many deer. Tribe need meat. My hunters kill deer and skin them. Tanned by our women. None better," Red Hawk said, nodding.

"That is why I seek to trade with you. The shops in Charles Town want good skins such as these. How many do you have?" Francis asked, his voice taking on a businesslike tone. He knew he had to negotiate a fair deal for both sides.

"Have many. One hundred twenty skins. All strong and thick. My people work hard. Want good trade," Red Hawk replied, gesturing to the bundles of deerskins.

Francis examined the skin again. "Yes, the quality is fine. But that many skins is a large haul. I must be careful. Such numbers take time to sell. What do you ask in return?"

"We need muskets, flints, and powder. And knives and hatchets. Also, cloth, bright like sunrise."

"Muskets, flint, and powder? That's a costly request. The King's men closely watch such dealings. I can offer iron tools, fine knives, and cloth in various colors, including red, blue, and even yellow. But only a few muskets with flints and a little powder," Francis countered.

"We are warriors. We need muskets to defend land. And to hunt. You bring little; we trade little."

Francis paused, reflecting on Red Hawk's words. "I respect your needs, Red Hawk. I'll provide more powder—but only if you agree to fewer muskets. Powder is easier to transport without alerting the King's men."

With narrowed eyes, Red Hawk replied, nodding, "More powder good. But need ten muskets."

"Ten is too many," countered Francis, shaking his head. "I can offer five muskets with flints and powder for all the skins, and I'll add a barrel of sugar and some extra cloth—your women will like that."

Red Hawk considered the offer. "You sly like fox, Locke. Eight muskets with flints, extra powder, sugar, and more cloth. And tobacco. Then we have deal."

"A hard bargain, Red Hawk! Tobacco too. We have a deal," Francis said with a laugh, extending his hand.

"We trade today and maybe again. But remember: trader who cheats no trade again," Red Hawk cautioned as he clasped Locke's hand.

"I trade fairly, Red Hawk. May our business be long and prosperous," Francis said, smiling.

Francis returned from the Catawba camp and guided the wagon toward the barn on his farm. Matthew was standing in the doorway, waiting for him. "Matthew, I just bought one hundred and twenty deerskins from Red Hawk in exchange for eight muskets, flints, powder, sugar, cloth, and tobacco," Francis announced. "We need to take them to Charles Town next week to trade for those items, plus goods we can trade with the Moravians."

Matthew picked up a deerskin, running his fingers over the soft hide. "These are fine skins. They should be well received in Charles Town."

"Yes, they should," Francis agreed.

At daybreak on Monday morning, the brothers loaded provisions onto the wagon carrying the deerskins, hitched the horses to the wagon, and set out for Charles Town in the colony of South Carolina. The trip covered about 250 miles and took five days. Each evening at sunset, they stopped to camp, care for the horses, and rest before continuing at first light the next day.

One morning, after breaking camp and starting on their way, their journey was interrupted. As they rounded a curve, five Native American warriors on horseback, with bows drawn, blocked the road. Matthew pulled the reins to stop the wagon, and Francis jumped down.

"Let us pass," ordered Francis as he approached the warriors, his hand resting on his pistol in his belt.

"This Santee land." One warrior said. "Need trade something to pass."

"We have nothing to trade."

"Then you not pass," the warrior said.

"We are going to Charles Town. If you let us pass, we will bring tobacco back for you."

The warrior hesitated momentarily, eyeing Francis's hand on his pistol. "You may pass now. If no bring tobacco, then we take horses."

"Deal," Francis replied as he got onto the wagon.

The warriors rode to the side of the road, allowing Francis and Matthew to pass.

"Whew! That was a close one," Matthew exclaimed.

"Yes, I'm sure they will be waiting for us when we return. We will need to have some tobacco for them."

Arriving at a small trading post on the outskirts of Charles Town, South Carolina, the two got down from their wagon and took a deerskin inside.

Ian Whitaker, the owner, was standing behind the counter. Ian was a short, stout man with a red beard and hair tied back, dressed in knickers and stockings, with a shopkeeper's apron tied around his waist.

The wooden shop was stocked with bolts of cloth, iron tools, muskets, powder horns, and other valuable manufactured goods from England. With tensions rising between the British and French over the Ohio River Valley, supplies had become more expensive, making trade negotiations critical.

Francis approached the counter and laid down the deerskin. "Good day, sir. My name is Francis Locke, and this is my brother, Matthew. We've got some deerskins you might be interested in."

Mr. Whitaker eyed the deerskin. "Good day, gentlemen. My name is Ian Whitaker. That is a fine skin. Freshly tanned, I see. How many do you have for me today?"

"A hundred and twenty prime skins, all well-cured. I reckon the softest doeskins among them will make fine ladies' gloves," Francis offered.

Matthew added, "And not a mite of insect damage or rough handling. We took great care, Mr. Whitaker. These are worth a fair price in trade."

"They are good quality, no doubt. But with the French stirring up trouble in the backcountry, English goods are harder to come by. I can offer you powder, flints, and shot, but I cannot spare much fine cloth or muskets," offered Mr. Whitaker.

"We need muskets and lead more than anything. Powder and flints, too. No use having powder or flints without muskets," Francis said.

"And we've got kinfolk needing cloth - good wool for the cold months and linen for shirts. You've got some, I see," Matthew said, looking around the shop.

Mr. Whitaker leaned against the counter and objected, "Cloth is scarce. The ships from England don't come as often as they should because of the war with France. I'll give you one musket with flint and powder, two lengths of wool, and ten yards of linen for twenty pelts."

Francis shook his head. "That's too steep. We'll give you ten pelts, but no more." "Ten pelts for one musket with flint and powder, two yards of wool, and ten yards of linen, and I'll throw in some iron tools. I need to clear room in my storehouse," Mr. Whitaker said, scratching his chin.

"We could use a few hatchets and knives. But we'll need lead too—enough to last a season's hunting," Matthew said.

"I'll give you a half-stone of lead shot with each musket, flints, powder, one hatchet, one knife, two lengths of wool, and ten yards of linen for twelve pelts," Mr. Whitaker countered. Francis exchanged glances with Matthew.

"Twelve muskets, flints, powder, lead, twenty-four yards of wool, 120 yards of linen, and iron tools for our 120 skins. It's a deal if you throw in a barrel of sugar and a hogshead of tobacco."

Mr. Whitaker paused momentarily as he looked directly at Francis, sizing him up and mentally determining if this would be a good deal. "You are a shrewd dealer, Mr. Locke," he said, extending his hand. "You've got a deal. Shake on it."

"Shake on it," Francis said, gripping Whitaker's hand.

"Let's pack up our goods now. We have a long journey ahead, and the French have been riling up the Indians against the British. Best not to stay in town too long," Matthew said as the two turned and made their way toward the door.

The narrow dirt road winding through the Carolina backcountry was quiet except for the creaking of wagon wheels and the rhythmic clop of horses' hooves. With reins in hand, Matthew glanced at Francis, sitting beside him on the wagon seat, his musket at the ready. The two, weary from their long journey, were eager to reach home before nightfall.

"This is the same area where those Santee warriors stopped us last week," Matthew said as his hands tightened on the reins.

"Yep," Francis answered. "Shouldn't be long now."

Sure enough, as they came over a slight rise, the five warriors were waiting for them in the middle of the road. As Matthew stopped the horses and pulled the brake handle back, Francis jumped from the wagon, walked to the back, and returned with five bundles of tobacco.

He approached the warriors and handed the bundles to one of them. "Here is the tobacco I promised."

The warrior took the bundles and handed one to each of the other warriors. "You may pass. You honest man. I will remember."

"Thank you," Francis replied as he returned to the wagon and climbed on.

As the warriors moved out of the way, Matthew shook the reins to get the horses moving and said, "I reckon we ought to press on faster."

"I agree," Francis murmured, eyes scanning the thick vegetation along the road. "These parts are not known for their hospitality after dark."

Matthew nodded and shook the reins again to urge the horses forward. Their wagon was laden with goods, enough to attract unwanted attention.

About an hour later, as the road passed through a low, swampy area, the sudden rustle in the underbrush was their only warning. Two figures burst onto the road ahead, their faces hidden by scarves and their pistols raised.

"Hold it right there!" one of them barked. "Throw down your weapons and step down from the wagon!"

Matthew tightened his grip on the reins, his mind racing. Francis, steady as stone, raised his musket.

"I will not say that again," the bandit said as he pointed his pistol toward Francis.

"There's no need for bloodshed, gentlemen," Francis said, his voice calm.

"There will be no trouble if you just throw down your weapons and step down from that wagon!" the second bandit demanded.

As the first bandit shifted his pistol, finger tightening on the trigger, Francis quickly aimed his musket and fired. The shot rang out, echoing through the trees. The bandit staggered back, clutching his side and cursing. Matthew, seizing the moment, cracked the whip. The horses lunged forward as the stunned bandits jumped out of the way. As the wagon lunged past, the second bandit fired wildly, his shot splintering the wood on the back of the wagon but missing its intended target. Francis pulled out his pistol, turned, and fired again—this time, the second bandit dove for cover in the underbrush, cursing. The wounded bandit, realizing his disadvantage, scrambled after his partner, vanishing into the brush. Francis and Matthew didn't stop. Matthew urged the horses into a hard gallop, the wagon bouncing violently along the uneven road.

It wasn't until the glow of a distant fire marked the outskirts of a settlement that he finally slowed the horses, his grip on the reins slick with sweat.

Matthew exhaled, shaking his head from side to side. "Well, that was a bit more excitement than I wanted."

Francis sighed and let out a chuckle. "I agree wholeheartedly."

The brothers rode on, now able to laugh at this potential disaster, their wagon still laden with goods. When they arrived back at the barn on Francis's farm, they unhitched the horses and led them into their stalls. Then, they pulled the wagon into the wagon shed and closed the doors for the night. The two men stood outside the barn, plotting their next move.

"Tomorrow, I will take the goods that I traded them for to the Catawba camp. The day after tomorrow, let's take some of these goods to the Moravian settlement at Salem for trading," Francis said.

The next day, Francis returned to the Catawba camp with eight muskets, flints, powder, sugar, cloth, and tobacco. As Francis halted his wagon in front of Red Hawk's lodge, several Native American women and children hurried over eagerly.

Red Hawk, seated on a log, stood up. "Greetings, Locke."

"Greetings, Red Hawk," Francis replied. "Here are the goods we agreed upon in exchange for the deerskins."

"Thank you," Red Hawk said, and the two men began unloading the wagon together.

"These fine muskets," Red Skin said as he admired the guns. "My warriors will be happy."

"Now you can get more deerskins for me!" Francis replied.

Red Hawk laughed at that comment.

After the wagon was unloaded, Red Hawk said, "We will have more deerskins for you by first snow."

"I will be back then," Francis replied as he mounted the wagon to return home.

The Moravian town of Salem was a half-day wagon ride from Salisbury. When the brothers arrived, they stopped at a trading post and entered through the front door. The aroma of freshly cut wood and leather filled the air. Handmade furniture was on display throughout the room, and the wooden counters displayed finely crafted pottery and leather goods. Brother Elias, a Moravian shopkeeper and craftsman, was standing behind the counter in black trousers, a white shirt, and a black vest. A narrow-brimmed black hat covered his brown hair, which was tied back.

He greeted the brothers with a measured nod. "Greetings, gentlemen. How may I help you?"

"Good day, sir. My name is Francis Locke from Salisbury, and this is my brother, Matthew. We have fine wool and linen cloth from England, sturdy iron tools, and even a small amount of sugar from the West Indies for trade. These items are valuable to a growing settlement like yours."

"Good day. I am Brother Elias. Indeed, such goods are always useful. But we trade fairly and with careful measure. Our brethren have labored hard on the items you see here—furniture, leather goods, and pottery. What do you wish to trade for them?"

"We are interested in your furniture, especially tables and chairs, as well as leather boots, belts, and saddles. Your Moravian craftsmen are known for their fine work, and such goods are in demand in both Charles Town and Salisbury," Francis replied.

"We would also be interested in your fine pottery—folks in the backcountry always need durable wares," Matthew added.

"A fair request. Let us speak in terms. Our community particularly needs wool and linen cloth, as we must clothe many. Our carpenters and furniture makers can also use iron tools. And we use sugar for baking and medicinal purposes."

"Then we have an opportunity for fair trade. We propose two tables and eight chairs for twenty yards of wool cloth. Two pairs of boots and a saddle for eight pounds of iron tools," Francis replied.

"And for the sugar, perhaps three sets of pottery?" Matthew offered.

Brother Elias leaned on the counter and paused, mentally tallying the offer. "That is a generous offer, but skilled hands made these goods with great care. I would ask for twenty-five yards of wool for the furniture. The boots and saddle we shall trade for ten pounds of iron tools. As for the sugar, two pottery sets will be fair."

Francis paused and stroked his chin. "You drive a hard bargain, Brother Elias. But twenty-five yards of wool cloth is too much. Shall we meet in the middle at twenty-two?"

Brother Elias considered the counteroffer for a moment, then nodded. "Agreed."

"And the rest stands?" Matthew asked.

"It does," Brother Elias replied.

"Then we have a deal," Francis said, extending his hand to shake and seal the deal.

Several Moravian craftsmen carefully loaded the furniture, pottery, and leather goods onto the wagon while the English cloth, iron tools, and sugar were meticulously counted, weighed, and stored. Francis, Matthew, and Brother Elias were pleased—a fair trade had been concluded in good faith.

As Francis and Matthew were about to climb onto the wagon for the return trip to Salisbury, Francis turned and asked, "Can you tell me where we might find Brother Mathias? We met him on the Great Wagon Road several years ago while traveling together. Also in his group were a Brother Samuel and a Sister Ann."

"Brother Mathias has a house just down the road. It's a clapboard house painted white, with a white picket fence in front. You will find him there," Brother Elias said. "Sister Ann is his wife."

"Thank you, sir. We will stop there on our way out of town."

As Francis and Matthew stopped their wagon in front of Brother Mathias's house, Sister Ann, sweeping the front steps, welcomed them. "Greetings, friends! It has been a long time since we traveled from Pennsylvania. I trust you arrived at your destination safely and all is well!"

"Greetings, Sister Ann! Yes, we arrived safely, and all is well," replied Francis as he climbed down from the wagon. "We have a farm just west of Salisbury. Brother Mathias told us we would be welcome here, and he also said that we might get some of your fine cheese!"

Hearing the conversation between his wife and Francis, Brother Mathias stepped out of the front door of the house. "Greetings,

Francis and Matthew! It's good to see you, and you're obviously doing well! I have a fresh wheel of fine cheddar that you may have."

"We would gladly pay you for it," Francis countered.

"That will not be necessary. Consider it a gift for an old friend."

"You are too kind, sir. Thank you."

After catching up and bidding farewell to Brother Mathias and Sister Ann, Francis carefully placed the wrapped wheel of cheese in the wagon, shook the reins, and he and Matthew made their way back to Salisbury.

The two brothers expanded their trading network over the next several years by profitably transporting goods between Native American tribes, as well as between Salisbury, Charles Town, and Salem. They built strong relationships with the Native Americans, merchants, farmers, and craftsmen along the route, allowing them to exchange various goods, including firearms, textiles, tools, and agricultural products. As their business grew, they invested in more wagons and hired workers to meet the rising demand. Their trade ventures brought them financial success and established them as key figures in the regional economy, linking inland settlements with the bustling port city of Charles Town.

10
Conflict and Politics

In 1758, the French and Indian War was raging. While most fighting took place in the northern colonies, settlers in the southern colonies still faced the threat of attacks from Native Americans, keeping most colonists on alert.

That spring, Francis was plowing a field to get ready for planting corn when a rider approached. Francis pulled the straps to stop the horse pulling the plow.

"Are you Francis Locke?" asked the rider as he dismounted and walked toward Francis.

"Yes, sir, I am," Francis replied, laying the plow down and brushing dust off his pants as he approached the rider.

"I have a letter for you, sir," the rider said, handing Francis a paper.

"Thank you, sir."

Francis examined the return address and noticed it was from Governor Arthur Dobbs in New Bern. As he would soon discover, this letter was about to alter the course of his life.

"You're welcome. Good day to you, sir," the rider replied, then mounted his horse and rode away.

Francis broke the official seal, opened the letter, and read it:

> *8 May 1758*
> *Mister Francis Locke*
> *Rowan County*
> *The Colony of North Carolina*
>
> *Dear Mr. Locke:*
>
> *I am pleased to inform you that I am appointing you as an ensign in the Rowan County, North Carolina, militia, commanded by Captain Griffith Rutherford. You are ordered to report to Captain*

Rutherford at militia headquarters on Main Street, Salisbury, North Carolina, on 15 May 1758.

His Excellency, Governor Arthur Dobbs

As Francis returned home from the fields later that day, he showed Anna the letter. "A rider brought this to me today. It seems I've been conscripted into the militia."

"Oh no! I read in the North Carolina Gazette that the British are at war with the French. Does that mean you will have to go fight the French?" Anna asked with a worried look.

"I will not know until I report to Captain Rutherford," Francis answered. "It all depends on what will be required of the militia. Right now, that conflict is mainly in Virginia and the northern colonies."

"Oh, I hope you don't have to go fight. I will worry about you! You could get hurt or be killed! And it's planting season. What will we do if you can't get the crops in the fields?"

"If I must go, I will hire some workers to plant the crops."

On May 15, Francis tied his horse outside the militia headquarters in Salisbury and took off his hat as he walked inside. About twenty men were seated and standing around the room. Captain Rutherford sat behind a desk in the back, studying a map.

Francis approached the desk and said to Captain Rutherford, "Good day, sir. I am Francis Locke, reporting for duty, as ordered."

"Good day, Ensign Locke. I'll address the men shortly, so please stand by."

"Yes, sir," replied Francis as he bowed and turned to join the other men.

Several other men came in over the next fifteen minutes and checked in.

Shortly, Captain Rutherford rose and addressed the men. "Men, the French have allied with several Indian tribes to take control of parts of America, mainly in the northern colonies. Therefore, England has declared war on France. Governor Dobbs has formed this Rowan County regiment of the North Carolina Militia and appointed me as its commander. The Cherokee and Catawba are aligned with the English, so I don't expect any major conflicts here in North Carolina. Our primary concern is whether we will need to support the conflict in Virginia or the northern colonies. Meanwhile, we will train and prepare as best we can. You will need to bring your own arms and ammunition. We will meet tomorrow at 7:00 AM at my farm, about seven miles north, to start our training. That's all."

That evening around the supper table, Francis told Anna about the meeting and that he would be training with the militia.

"Oh, Francis, I am so worried!" Anna exclaimed as she served her husband some corn and chicken. "If something were to happen to you, I don't know what I would do!"

"I understand, Anna, but I have to do what I can to protect you and the children and preserve our way of life."

"I know, but I'll still worry! And I'll pray for your safety!"

"We are just going to train for now. The militia might not even be deployed," Francis said as he took a bite of chicken.

"I just hope that will be all. I love you, and I can't bear to be without you."

"I know. I love you too. Now stop worrying and eat your supper."

Francis and about 100 other militia members gathered at the Rutherford farm the next morning, as ordered. The intense drills included target practice, hand-to-hand combat training, and close-order marching. The militia trained each week for the rest of the year, sharpening its skills and preparing for the possibility of battle. Although they never saw action in the French and Indian War, Francis served honorably and gained valuable experience in leadership and combat strategies that would benefit him in the years to come.

During his time as an ensign in the militia, Francis continued to run the transport company with his brother, manage his farm, plant and harvest crops, and, more importantly, focus on his wife, Anna, and their three young children: Rebecca, 4; John, 3; and Polly, 2.

In August 1760, Francis and Matthew came back from a trip to Charles Town with a load of muskets, powder, linen cloth, and iron tools. As they neared Francis's farm, James rode up to them quickly and stopped his horse amid a cloud of dust.

James jumped down from his horse with tears in his eyes. "I have some terrible news! Your mother is not well! We need to ride to her house immediately!"

As Francis and Matthew entered the bedroom, their mother, Eliza, was in bed, holding her head, moaning, sweating, and convulsing.

"Have you sent for the doctor?" Francis said with concern in his eyes.

"Yes, George went to fetch him. Hopefully, they will be here shortly."

"How long has she been like this?" Matthew asked.

"She was complaining of a severe headache late yesterday. It was so bad that she was vomiting and sweating throughout the night," Richard replied.

As the three sat beside Eliza, praying with tears in their eyes and waiting for the doctor to arrive, she suddenly became still. She opened her eyes, looked at them with a smile, and exhaled her last breath.

When the doctor arrived and examined her, his only words were, "I'm sorry. She's gone."

"Why?" Francis asked, still teary-eyed.

"Evidently, from her headache, sweating, and vomiting, an artery in her brain ruptured, causing bleeding in the brain," the doctor answered. "I am so sorry for your loss."

As expected, the funeral service was a somber occasion because of her unexpected passing. Her family and many friends attended. Elizabeth Brandon, affectionately called Eliza, was laid to rest in the cemetery at Thyatira Presbyterian Church beside her husband, Richard.

◆ ◆ ◆

"I'm home, dear!" Francis said as he returned from Charles Towne one evening in 1763. "And I have some great news!"

"I'm so glad you're home!" Eliza replied, giving her husband a hug and a kiss. "What is the good news?"

"The talk around Charles Town is that the French have surrendered control to the English and signed a peace treaty in Paris."

"That *is* great news! That means you won't have to go fight anywhere!"

"Exactly!"

"Are you hungry?"

"I am starving. It feels good to be home!"

"Go wash up. Supper's almost ready. Children, come to the table."

After supper, Francis and Anna sat by the fireplace, enjoying each other's company while their children—Rebecca, 9, John, 8, Polly, 7, and William, 5—played on the floor. One-year-old Margaret was already in bed.

"Anna, I've been thinking," Francis said, leaning back in his rocking chair.

Anna, working on her knitting, paused briefly and looked at Francis with raised eyebrows. "Oh? About what?"

"Being on the road to Charles Town all the time wears on me and keeps me away from you and the children. When I am home, I work in the fields day after day, and it's hard, exhausting work. I'm thinking about opening a tavern."

Why would he want to do such a thing? she thought as she laid down her knitting and looked into his eyes.

"I *would* like to have you home more, and I know working the fields is hard. Do you know how to manage a tavern?" Anna asked.

Francis tossed another log on the fire and settled back in his chair. "There's nothing complicated about running a tavern. I know how to serve beer and whiskey, and I understand how to run a business and handle money. I'm outgoing and enjoy talking with people. Farming is hard work, and I'm not getting any younger.

"Managing a tavern would allow me to slow down a bit, and with the money I earn, I could hire help to tend to the fields. This would also allow me to meet more of the men in the county and get involved in local issues. I can only meet people and discuss current events now when I go to Salisbury for supplies once a month."

"Francis, you have been a loving husband and a devoted father to the children, and I love you so much. You know I will support you no matter what you decide."

"Thank you, Anna. I love you, too."

By the end of the year, after Francis finished harvesting the crops, he applied for and received a license from Rowan County to run an ordinary at his home. He installed an entrance door on the side wall of the room in front of the library, set up a hitching post, and hung a sign advertising the tavern. He built a bar along the back wall, furnished the room with tables and chairs, ordered and stocked beer and whiskey, and announced that he was open for business. The tavern was an enormous success, attracting many regular customers.

One evening in 1765, while Francis was behind the bar, his brother Matthew entered the tavern. "Have you seen the latest issue of the North Carolina Gazette?"

Francis was restocking bottles of port wine on the back counter. "No, I haven't. Is there an article of particular interest?"

Matthew leaned against the counter. "There are two articles of particular interest. First, the British have imposed a tax on paper goods and legal documents. It's part of the Stamp Act. Every printed paper or legal document will be taxed between three and sixpence per sheet! Another article reports that the British Parliament has passed the Quartering Act, which states that colonies must provide housing and food for British troops!"

"Do they expect us to house and feed their troops?" Francis asked in disbelief. "Most folks can barely feed their own families, let alone some strange soldiers. And where will people house these troops? Most homesteads aren't that big!"

"This Act requires the colonial governors to find accommodations for soldiers, such as in barns and outbuildings. Fortunately, they are not required to provide housing in people's homes. I'm not sure how much more of this British tyranny we can tolerate," Matthew replied. "Also, on the back page is an article stating that the Virginia House of Burgesses has passed the Virginia Resolves, which are seven resolutions challenging the legality of the Stamp Act."

"I'm not sure if that will do any good. The British have tight control over the American colonies," Francis said.

At that moment, William Steele, a town commissioner of Salisbury, stepped into the tavern.

"Good evening, William. The usual?" Francis asked.

"Yes, please."

"Here you are," Francis said, placing a tankard of beer on the counter in front of William.

"Francis, I've been meaning to talk to you about something," William said, sipping his beer. "There's an opening for county sheriff. William Nassery has resigned, and I think you should consider that position. If you're interested, I can put in a good word for you with Judge Fanning."

Francis wiped the bar with a towel. "I'm honored that you would think of me for that position. Yes, I would be interested."

"Good. I will talk to Judge Fanning tomorrow," William replied as he finished his beer and put three shillings on the bar. "I need to head out since I have an early day tomorrow. I just wanted to stop by and see if being a sheriff interests you. Good evening."

"Good evening to you, and thank you."

Since Matthew had already left, there were no other patrons in the bar, and since it was late, Francis closed for the night.

◆◆◆

When Francis entered the sitting room, Anna was sitting by the fireplace, enjoying the warmth.

"William Steele was here at the tavern tonight, and he asked me if I was interested in becoming the sheriff of Rowan County," Francis said. "He mentioned that if I wanted that position, he would speak to Judge Fanning about appointing me."

Anna paused for a moment before speaking. "That's an important position; it would consume a lot of your time. Are you certain you want to be sheriff with everything going on in your life?"

"I think so. The county needs an honest person as sheriff, and I am honored to be considered. And I will be paid," Francis said as he pulled a chair closer to the fireplace and sat down.

Before replying, Anna wrapped a shawl around her shoulders and thought for a moment. "What are the duties of a sheriff?"

"Besides keeping the peace and occasionally testifying in court, one duty involves collecting taxes. The Regulators have been very vocal, protesting against unfair taxation and corruption among colonial officials. As sheriff, I would treat everyone fairly and honestly."

"That would be a welcome relief! It sounds like a great opportunity. If that's something you want to do, you have my support. Can you please add another log to the fire? I've got a chill."

Francis got up and added another log to the fire, then, before sitting back down, he leaned over, kissed Anna, and said, "Thank you, dear. I knew you would support me."

"Place your right hand on the Bible, raise your left hand, and repeat after me," Judge Fanning said as he began administering the oath to Francis as the new Rowan County sheriff. Francis took the oath and received a badge and card designating him as the sheriff of Rowan County.

One afternoon, Francis rode into a field where Jacob Schmidt was loading hay into a wagon. Francis dismounted his horse. "Good afternoon, Jacob."

Jacob recognized that this was not a social visit by the badge on Francis's coat. "Good afternoon, Francis," he said with a scowl.

"Jacob, I am here on official county business. As sheriff, I must inform you that you are delinquent in your taxes, which I am here to collect."

Jacob pointed his pitchfork directly at Francis. "Francis, you know as well as I do that the taxes imposed on the citizens of this county by the English are unfair. I will not pay them, and I suggest you leave my property before I have to use this pitchfork."

"Jacob, it is my duty to enforce the law. We've been friends for a long time, so I won't fight you. However, if you don't pay your taxes, I will have to seize your property."

"If you try to take my property, you'll have a fight on your hands. Now, get off my property, and don't come back!" Jacob ordered, placing the pitchfork within inches of Francis's chest.

Later that day, Francis stood before the judge, his hands clasped in front of him.

"Your Honor, I have not been able to collect any more taxes from the citizens of Rowan County because they believe the taxation imposed on them is unfair. Many citizens have violently opposed my efforts to either collect taxes from them or confiscate property for unpaid taxes or debts."

"Sheriff Locke, I understand your challenges, but you are sworn to uphold the law. The taxes need to be paid."

"Yes, your Honor. Even when I try to confiscate property for unpaid taxes or debts, I face violent resistance," Francis responded. "Last month, I seized a sorrel gelding belonging to James Dunlap for his unpaid taxes from '64, '65, and '66, but Dunlap and fifteen other men came to my farm and forcefully and unlawfully took back the horse."

The judge looked over some papers on his desk. "According to your records, you have only collected about one-third of all taxes owed in the county."

Francis wiped the sweat from his brow with a handkerchief. "That is correct, Your Honor. Many citizens have joined this Regulator Movement, believing the taxes they are being charged are excessive and unfair."

"Sheriff Locke, you know the law. Now go out there and do your duty," the judge said as he struck his gavel.

Francis continued to carry out his official duties and uphold the law to the best of his ability, despite facing ongoing resistance and occasional violent threats. In 1766, he resigned as sheriff of Rowan County to spend more time with his family, manage the tavern and farm, and pursue other interests in county politics.

In early June 1768, while Francis and his Negro man, Saipo, were feeding the horses and mucking out the stalls in his barn, Matthew rode up, reined his horse beside the barn, dismounted, and went inside. "Hello, Francis. How are you?"

"I'm doing well. How about you?"

"I'm doing well."

Francis leaned a pitchfork against the wall. "What brings you here today?"

"With my growing family, I need to add a room to my house, and I could definitely use your carpentry skills."

Francis poured feed from a bucket into a trough in a stall and looked at his brother with curiosity. "Alright, what do you have planned?"

"I want to add an extra bedroom to the back of the house," Matthew said as he sat on a stool.

Francis put the bucket down and sat on the feed bin beside his brother. "I'd be happy to help. Do you have plans?"

Matthew pulled a piece of paper out of his pocket. "I have a pencil sketch of what I want."

Francis examined the sketch as he stroked his chin. "It looks pretty straightforward. A 20-foot by 15-foot room at the back with two windows and a door into the house. Have you estimated and ordered the materials?"

"I've figured out how much lumber I need, but I haven't purchased it yet. We'll also need nails, shingles, paint, two windows, and a door."

"We can get lumber and shingles at the Moravian sawmill in Salem. Also, they craft beautiful windows and doors. We can pick those up there. As for the other materials, you can get those at Murdoch's hardware store in Salisbury."

"Great," Matthew replied. "Can you ride with me to Salem tomorrow?"

"Sure," Francis replied. "We can begin the addition to your house next week."

The next day, the two brothers headed to Salem to buy their first load of lumber, along with the windows and a door. Then, as they came back through Salisbury, they stopped at Murdoch's Hardware to pick up nails. They decided to purchase the lap siding, pine boards for the interior walls, shingles, and paint as needed.

After laying out the location of the addition with stakes and string, the brothers stacked stones at the corners, placed the band on the stone pillars, and nailed the joists to the band. Then, after ensuring the structure was level, they nailed down the pine flooring, framed and raised the walls, and built the roof, covering it with pine boards.

Francis set his hammer and nail pouch down and turned to Matthew. "We need to go back to Salem tomorrow to pick up the lap siding, shingles, and the pine boards for the interior walls. After we put on the lap siding and shingles, we'll cut an opening in the back of your house for the door to the new room."

Returning from Salem, the brothers got to work and finished the roof and exterior by the following week. They then installed the boards on the interior walls. The only thing left was painting, which Matthew finished by late July.

"It's a beautiful room, and we needed the extra space," Mary Elizabeth, Matthew's wife, exclaimed as she admired the new area. "Thank you, Francis, for your help!"

"You're welcome," Francis said as he packed up his tools. "I know you will enjoy it."

"We certainly will!" Mary Elizabeth exclaimed as she walked around and admired her new room.

As James Patton, a Rowan County commissioner, entered the tavern one evening in 1770, Francis greeted him, "Good evening, James. The usual?"

"Yes, sir," James replied as he walked up to the bar. "Francis, there's a job opening with the county. Are you interested?"

"What kind of job?" Francis asked as he placed a tankard of beer in front of James.

"The primary duty of the position would be as County Coroner. However, that role does not require much work, as it only comes into play during suspicious deaths in the county, which are relatively infrequent. Also, this position would oversee the surveying and construction of roads and bridges, and occasionally fill in for the jailer."

"How much does it pay?" Francis asked.

"Twenty shillings per day, but you would only be paid for the days you work."

"I am interested. How do I apply?" Francis asked.

"You can apply at the Rowan County offices in Salisbury," James replied. "Thank you, James. I will stop by tomorrow," Francis said as he wiped the bar counter with a towel.

The next day, Francis applied for the county job, was hired, and served in that role for several years. He played a vital part in making sure roads and bridges built in the county were passable and safe, and he sometimes performed the duties of county coroner with care and respect for the families involved.

11
Early Actions in the War

In late summer 1774, Matthew walked into the tavern one evening. "Good evening, Francis," he said, approaching the bar. "Good evening, Matthew. How are you?"

"I'm mad as a hornet! I'm fed up with British officials treating us like second-class citizens. The excessive taxation, stricter regulations on trade, and now English troops are showing up to enforce the King's laws."

"I agree," Francis replied. "There's a lot of unrest and dissatisfaction, not just here in Rowan County but throughout North Carolina and other colonies. Would you like a beer?"

"Yes, please."

Francis slid a tankard of beer across the bar to his brother. "There have even been some minor skirmishes between the Loyalists and the Patriots here. Did you hear about what happened in Boston last year? The British have imposed martial law there because a group of Patriots dressed as Indians dumped tea in the harbor to protest unfair taxation."

Matthew sipped his beer. "Yes, I have heard about what people are calling the Boston Tea Party! Many people are talking about independence from England. Even last month in Edenton, Penelope Barker, the wife of Thomas Barker, the Treasurer of the Province of North Carolina, convinced around fifty women to sign a petition protesting British trade regulations. Those women resolved to stop drinking tea and buying English clothes as a protest against taxation without representation. They are calling this the Edenton Tea Party!"

Francis handed a glass of port to another customer, wiped down the bar, and went back to Matthew. "Yes, I have heard of the Edenton Tea Party. They didn't dump any tea like in Boston, but that was a bold display of patriotism."

"Also, the Quartering Act of 1765 has been amended to require British troops to be housed in private homes and facilities!" Matthew said. "Can you believe that!"

Francis looked directly at Matthew, raising his voice in anger. "If they try to house British soldiers in my home, they'll have a fight on their hands!"

"I have some good news," Matthew said. "Last year, the Continental Congress authorized the creation of Committees of Safety, and the Second North Carolina Provincial Congress endorsed it. The first meeting of the Rowan County Committee of Safety took place last night. I've been elected to join them."

"You're treading on dangerous ground," Francis replied. "Going against the King of England is a treasonous offense, punishable by death. But I cannot say I blame you."

"We cannot continue to live this way. I do hope you will join us."

Francis served a beer to another patron and wiped down the bar in front of Matthew. "You are my brother, and I will support you, Matthew. The British have become tyrants in their oppressive and absolute authority."

"You're correct, Francis. We've been through a lot together. We will survive this, too. Thank you for the beer. I must take my leave. Say 'Hi' to Anna for me," Matthew said as he laid three shillings on the bar and headed for the door.

Early one morning in June 1775, Matthew reined his horse in front of Francis and Anna's house and went inside.

"Good morning, Matthew. What brings you here so early? Would you like some coffee?" Francis asked as he welcomed Matthew into the dining room.

"Good morning. Are you out of tea?"

"We are not drinking tea anymore in protest," Francis replied with a grin.

"Yes, coffee would be nice," Matthew said. Then, handing a newspaper to Francis, he asked, "Have you seen the latest copy of the North Carolina Gazette?"

"No, I haven't," Francis replied as he handed Matthew a mug of coffee and started reading the front-page article featuring the full text of the Mecklenburg Resolves.

"This declares that all laws and edicts issued by His Majesty are now void, and anyone who supports the English or their authorities will be considered an enemy of the country. We are heading toward war with England!"

"Oh, I hope not," Anna interrupted as she entered the room and sat at the table.

"You're correct, brother," Matthew said, sipping his coffee. "It also grants all legislative and executive authority to the Provincial Congress. Governor Josiah Martin has fled the state to a British man-of-war off the coast."

Francis poured himself another cup of coffee. "He needed to leave."

"I'm worried about where this is heading," Anna said, pouring herself a cup of coffee. "If there is a war, we cannot compete with the most powerful army in the world. I love you both, and I'm afraid of losing either of you in the fighting that would follow."

Matthew slowly set his coffee cup on the table, looking pensive. "That may be true, Anna, but we can't live under this tyranny. We must rise up and fight!"

"I know, but I can still worry!" Anna replied.

Matthew continued, "Now, for some news about me: The Committee on Safety has chosen me to represent Rowan County at the Third North Carolina Provincial Congress. We will meet in Hillsborough in August."

"That is quite an honor, Matthew. I'm so proud of you," Francis replied.

Matthew finished his coffee and stood up. "One of the agenda items we will address is dividing the state into military districts and organizing militias in those districts. I believe Salisbury will be one district. I can mention your name if you're interested in a leadership role."

Francis and Anna stood and walked Matthew to the door. "Thank you. I'm very interested, so please do."

"Oh, I almost forgot," Matthew said as he stopped at the door. "Last night, the Committee on Safety met at the courthouse in Salisbury and passed a resolution similar to the Mecklenburg Resolves, called the Rowan Resolves. It's entitled *Resolutions by inhabitants of Rowan County concerning resistance to Parliamentary taxation and the Provincial Congress of North Carolina.* That will certainly stir up the hornet's nest!"

After Matthew left, tears welled up in Anna's eyes. "Francis, are you sure you want to lead a militia regiment against the Loyalists and the British Army? That is the most powerful army in the world! You could end up badly wounded, imprisoned, or even worse—you could be killed!"

"I cannot sit still while my brother, other family members, and neighbors risk their lives for freedom from this tyranny. Yes, I'm sure. I want to do my part, and I will accept command of a regiment if offered."

Anna stood silently, crying and worrying about what the future held for her husband, family, and their way of life. Francis took her in his arms, kissed her tenderly, and assured her that everything would be fine.

The Third North Carolina Provincial Congress convened in Hillsborough in August 1775, with Matthew serving as a delegate from Rowan County. The Congress subdivided the state into six military districts: Edenton, Halifax, Hillsborough, New Bern, Salisbury, and Wilmington. Matthew nominated Francis for a leadership position in the Salisbury district, so Francis was appointed lieutenant colonel of the Rowan County Regiment of the North Carolina militia (Minutemen) under the command of Colonel Griffith Rutherford.

The Battle of Ninety Six

During a commissioning ceremony in Salisbury on November 1, 1775, in front of his officers, Colonel Rutherford pinned a lieutenant colonel patch onto Francis's lapel. "Francis Locke, you are now commissioned as a lieutenant colonel of the Rowan County Regiment of the North Carolina Militia. Congratulations."

Francis saluted and then shook Colonel Rutherford's hand. "Thank you, sir."

Colonel Rutherford then turned to the other officers. "Gentlemen, I have just received a message from Major Andrew Williamson of the Ninety Six District Regiment in South Carolina. The colonial government of South Carolina sent a shipment of weapons and ammunition to the town of Ninety Six. A large force of Loyalists is enroute to the town and is requesting immediate support. Notify your men that they must bring their own arms and ammunition. We will have several wagons to transport gear, food, and supplies. Your men may find this campaign challenging, as it is our first, and they might not be accustomed to a march of this nature. Because of the cold weather and rough terrain, the march will be long and arduous. We will leave tomorrow at dawn."

"Colonel," Francis said, "I am familiar with that area of South Carolina. Ninety-six is not far off the road to Charles Town, which I often traveled when I ran my transport company."

"Go on…," Colonel Rutherford replied.

"There are several good places where we can camp, and I also know of a few shortcuts that can save us some time."

"Excellent," Colonel Rutherford replied.

That evening, Francis broke the news to Anna at home. "I have been commissioned as a lieutenant colonel of the Rowan County Regiment of the North Carolina Militia. We have been requested to assist Loyalists guarding weapons and ammunition in the town of Ninety Six, South Carolina. So, I will be leaving tomorrow."

"Oh, no! How long will you be gone?" Anna asked, with tears in her eyes.

"That's hard to say. At least two weeks. Maybe more."

"Oh, Francis, I will worry constantly while you're away! Promise me you will be safe and return to me!"

"I promise. I love you very much. Please keep me and the men in your prayers."

"I love you, too. I know you have no choice, but I will still worry!"

"This is only the beginning of a long struggle for freedom, I fear. I have an early start tomorrow. Shall we go to bed?"

"Yes, I need to snuggle with you and have you hold me tight. It may be some time before you're back home!"

The Rowan County Regiment began its march to South Carolina at dawn the following day. The officers rode on horseback while the troops marched on foot. As the light of day faded, the regiment stopped to set up camp for the night. The officers had their own tents, while the men slept in four-man tents. There was also a large headquarters tent where the officers met, equipped with a portable desk and chair for Colonel Rutherford and a few chairs for the officers. Many of the men were unaccustomed to a march of this kind, and by the end of the first day, they were hungry, cold, and exhausted.

That night, around the officers' campfire, Francis asked, "Colonel Rutherford, do you have any intelligence you can share with us about what we will encounter when we arrive?"

"I cannot predict what kind of fighting we will encounter. I know that Major Williamson has constructed temporary fortifications near the town to safeguard a cache of weapons and ammunition. The Ninety Six District Regiment is at risk of being vastly outnumbered and losing the cache to the Loyalists without our support.

"Thank you, sir. I will relay that information to the men."

"We will break camp at first light and continue the march," Colonel Rutherford said. "Let's get some rest."

With that said, the men turned in for the night.

After a four-day journey, stopping only at night, they arrived at the fortifications built by Major Williamson near the town of Ninety Six. Major Williamson was seated behind his portable desk in the command tent when Colonel Rutherford and Francis entered, introducing themselves.

The major rose and saluted them. "Welcome to Williamson's Fort. We are still working on the fortifications. We expect a significant Loyalist force to arrive any day now."

Colonel Rutherford and Francis returned the salute and took their seats.

"Thank you, Major. We are here to assist in any way we can," offered Colonel Rutherford.

"Major, where are the Loyalists now?" Francis asked.

"My scouts have reported that they are a day's march from the town. Once they have secured the town, I expect them to attack us here."

"How many Loyalists are there?"

"About 1,800," the major replied.

"Major," Francis said, "Our men are mostly farmers and shopkeepers. Although they have had some training, they have no experience in fighting. They are tired and cold from the march, and their only ammunition is what they are carrying. I don't have a good feeling about our success, but we will do our best."

"Understood. All we can do is try. We are fighting for freedom," the major replied.

The following day, the Loyalists took control of the town of Ninety Six and began a siege of the Patriot position at Williamson's Fort. The battle was fierce and lasted three days, marked by intense cannon and musket fire, primarily from fortified positions behind houses, barns, and trees.

Facing a significant shortage of gunpowder, the Patriots, fearing Loyalist reinforcements could arrive at any moment, requested a ceasefire, which the Loyalists agreed to. The Loyalists withdrew, allowing the Patriots to dismantle their position and retreat without further conflict.

The Snow Campaign

As snow fell and the Rowan County Regiment was preparing to return home, Colonel Rutherford addressed his officers inside the command tent: "Gentlemen, I have been appointed to lead the newly established 1st Salisbury District Minutemen."

He then turned to Francis and said, "Lieutenant Colonel Locke, you are now commissioned as Colonel/Commandant of the newly formed 1st Rowan County Regiment of Militia. Congratulations."

"Thank you, sir," Francis replied.

After a round of applause from his officers, Colonel Rutherford continued, "Colonel Locke, you will lead your regiment to the mountains west of here to support the South Carolina Militia commanded by Colonel Richard Richardson in an attack on the Loyalist units camped in Indian Territory. The Loyalists are recruiting throughout the South Carolina backcountry and must be stopped. This action should be quick despite the freezing and snowy weather, as our combined forces will vastly outnumber the Loyalists."

Francis gathered his officers to share the news. "Gentlemen, I have just been promoted to colonel/commandant of the newly formed 1st Rowan County Regiment of Militia, of which you are part."

After a round of applause, Francis continued, "I am proud of the way you performed against the Loyalists here. Although they captured the weapons, our soldiers gained valuable combat experience, and I commend your leadership. Now, for the bad news: We have been ordered to support the South Carolina Militia, commanded by Colonel Richard Richardson, in an attack on the Loyalist units camped in Indian Territory west of here. We will leave tomorrow at dawn."

Colonel Locke's regiment began its westward march at daybreak the next day. As the Patriots reached the South Carolina regiment's camp at sundown, snow continued to fall, blanketing the ground with about eight inches.

Francis entered the headquarters tent and saluted Colonel Richardson. "Good evening, sir. I am Colonel Francis Locke with the 1st Rowan County Regiment of Militia. I have been ordered to support your efforts against the Loyalists here."

Colonel Richardson, studying a map on his desk, looked up and returned the salute. "Good evening, Colonel. Welcome to South Carolina. The Loyalists have been actively recruiting in this area. Our mission is to identify the leaders and undermine their efforts. I expect little difficulty. We will have a significant advantage: with my 1,300 troops, we outnumber them nearly five to one, especially with your troops added. I'm trying to determine the best route in this snowy weather!"

Francis sat down and looked at the map. "We are here, and the Loyalists' camp has been reported here," Francis said, pointing to two locations.

Then, pointing to another spot on the map, Francis said, "I think the best route into Indian Territory would be to cross the Saluda River here at Weaver's Ferry."

"Excellent," Colonel Richardson said. "We should be able to commandeer the ferry and move all the troops and equipment across the river in short order. From there, it should only be a quick march into Indian Territory."

The Patriot regiment reached Indian Territory on December 22nd, where they attacked Captain Patrick Cunningham's Loyalists' camp.

"Captain Armstrong, take your company to cover the right flank. Captain Cowan, take your company to the left. Captain Dixon and I will lead the rest of the companies up the middle," Francis ordered as his men advanced on the camp. "Fire at will, and be sure to take cover when you're reloading."

The ensuing battle was brief. Realizing they were outnumbered, Captain Cunningham yelled to his men, "We are outnumbered. Retreat and fend for yourselves!"

Approximately 150 Loyalists were captured, and six were killed. Captain Cunningham escaped on horseback and hid at a camp at the Great Cane Break on the Reedy River, where he was later captured.

Loyalist Colonel Thomas Fletchall was found hiding in the hollow of a sycamore tree on Fair Forest Creek. He and other Loyalist prisoners were sent to Charles Town with a company of Patriots.

The night before they were to head back to North Carolina, Francis and several of his officers gathered around a campfire.

Francis sat on a log, warming his hands. "Men, we've chased the Loyalists deep into these woods. They are cold, hungry, and dejected. We have captured quite a few. I'm proud of your outstanding work in this frigid weather."

Lieutenant Colonel Matthew Brandon sat poking the fire. "You are correct, Colonel. I have heard that some of their men have deserted. They did not expect us to have such a powerful force."

"Loyalty to the King comes at a price. We've shown them what the North Carolina militia is capable of," Francis replied. "We are finished here, so we will head home tomorrow."

Nearby, a group of soldiers huddled around another campfire, eating jerky and stamping their feet against the cold.

Upon hearing the officers at the nearby fire, Private Wallace Alexander said, "Colonel Locke, I'm delighted we'll be pulling out tomorrow. I truly miss my family."

Francis nodded. "I miss mine, too, soldier. Get some rest tonight; you deserve it and need it for tomorrow's march home."

The following day, Colonel Richardson and Colonel Locke's armies began their march home. They were tired; their boots were worn out, and they were poorly clothed. To make matters worse, during the march home, it snowed for 30 hours, dumping nearly 2 feet of snow. The Snow Campaign was grueling, cold, and exhausting, but Francis and his men proved their worth in the face of adversity.

12
The Cherokee Expedition

In early January, with snow on the ground and the sun setting in the west, Francis, after a cold, exhausting march from the mountains of South Carolina, pulled his horse to a stop in front of his house and went inside. Anna was upstairs in the bedroom, folding clothes, so she didn't hear him come in. Not seeing her, Francis quietly put down his musket, hung his hat and coat on the coat rack, and tiptoed up the stairs to the bedroom.

Seeing her there, he quietly announced, "Anna. I'm home!" Startled to hear his voice, Anna looked up and rushed to him by the door, then threw herself into his arms. "I'm so glad you're home and safe! Have you missed me?"

"Oh, how I've missed you!" Francis said as he kissed her gently.

"You must be cold!" Anna said. "Let's go downstairs by the fire. You can get warm, and we can talk."

As they sat by the fire, enjoying its warmth, Francis shared with Anna everything that had happened in South Carolina. Anna told him all about the family gathering at Christmas and how the children and other family members had missed him so much.

"You must be hungry. What have you eaten while you were away?" Anna asked.

"Mainly jerky and hard biscuits. One man shot a deer on the way home, so I had some venison stew a couple of nights ago. Yes, I'm starving!"

"Saipo cooked some Brunswick stew in an iron pot over a fire outside last week. He used squirrel, rabbit, chicken, potatoes, and onions in it. It's excellent! Would you like some?"

"You're already making my mouth water. That sounds great!"

As Anna heated some stew in the kitchen for her husband, Francis relaxed by the fire, enjoying the warmth and feeling grateful to be home. After supper, the two went to bed. Francis was exhausted and fell asleep immediately. Anna snuggled next to him and drifted off, too, grateful that he was home safe.

In September 1776, Colonel Griffith Rutherford gathered his officers at his headquarters in Salisbury for a briefing. "Gentlemen," he began, "on July 4th, the Continental Congress in Philadelphia declared independence from Britain. We are now the United States of America! Copies of that declaration are being distributed throughout the colonies and will be on display in front of the courthouse in Salisbury later this month."

At that announcement, all the men cheered, clapped, and smiled.

"Also, I have been promoted to Brigadier General," Rutherford said.

Once again, the men cheered and applauded.

After the excitement subsided, Rutherford continued. "We are getting reports that the British and Loyalists have been inciting the Cherokee to raid our settlements in the mountains because they say our settlers are encroaching on their lands. Several settlements have been raided, with homes burned to the ground. Settlers have been wounded, and some have been killed. We are to coordinate with the militia from South Carolina and Georgia to retaliate against the Cherokee and secure the frontier and settlements there."

Our objectives are to locate and attack Cherokee advance units and villages, capture or disperse key Cherokee leaders and fighters to weaken their ability to regroup, and protect the settlers in the area. Are there questions?

"One question, sir. What Cherokee towns will we be attacking, and how long will this march be? My men will want to know," Francis asked.

"Good questions, Colonel Locke," General Rutherford replied as he shuffled through some papers and picked one up, examining it. "Our focus will be the Cherokee towns of Coweecho and Chota. These towns are about a four-day march from here. Any more questions?"

As no one else had questions, the briefing came to a close.

Francis quickly gathered his officers to share the news. "Gentlemen, I have good news and bad news. First, the good news: On July 4th, the Continental Congress in Philadelphia declared independence from Britain. We are now the United States of America! Copies of that declaration will be posted in front of the courthouse in Salisbury later this month."

After the cheering and back-slapping stopped, Francis continued, "Now for the bad news: We will leave on Monday morning on an extended campaign to quell a Cherokee uprising in the mountains. We will be marching to several Cherokee towns, about a four-day march from here. The march will be tough because we will be in mountainous terrain with dense forests, and we will cross multiple rivers. We must also stay alert for Cherokee attacks. Have your men prepare for this expedition and gather at dawn on Monday."

"Sir, why are we fighting the Cherokee?" Major Dobbins asked.

Francis replied, "The British and Loyalists have incited the Cherokee to raid our settlements in the mountains because our settlers are encroaching on their lands. If we do not put down this uprising, the Cherokee will keep attacking settlers there, and maybe even those in Rowan County."

◆◆◆

Returning home, Francis tied his horse to the hitching post and went inside. Anna was sitting in the front room. "I'll be leaving Monday morning again," he said.

"You're going again?" Anna asked with a disappointed look.

"I'm afraid so. The British have been inciting the Cherokee to raid settlers in the mountains. We will be going there to put a stop to it."

"I miss you *so much* when you're gone, and I fear you will be killed or injured. And the children miss you, too!"

In 1776, Francis and Anna had four children living at home: Margaret, 14; Ann, 12; Francis Jr., whom they called Frankie, 10; and Matthew, 6.

"I know. I miss being with you all as well. But I am fighting for our freedom and safety. We cannot let the Cherokee attack settlers in their area. If we do not do something, they could start attacking the settlers here in Rowan County."

"I'm just being selfish. I want you here with us, but I know you must do your part to keep us safe. Please promise me you will be careful."

"I promise. What's for supper?"

"I've got a pot roast with potatoes, carrots, and onions in a Dutch oven over the fire."

"That sounds good!"

"It'll be about an hour before it's ready."

"That will give me time to put the horse in a stall and feed and water him," Francis said as he started out the door.

"Please feed the chickens, too," Anna replied.

Outside, Francis led his horse around back to the barn and put him in a stall. Then he went to the well, where he filled a bucket of water and took it back to the barn. After feeding and watering the horses, he threw some chicken feed down for the chickens. By the time he finished those chores, the sun had set, and the daylight was fading.

Walking back into the house, Francis went into the dining room and lit the candles on the table.

As Anna entered with a platter full of pot roast and vegetables, she called out, "Children, supper's ready. Come to the table!"

"That looks good!" Francis said as he took his seat, and the children filed in.

"Yes, it does!" Frankie replied, taking his place at the table. "I'm starving!"

Margaret took her place at the table. "Father, will you be staying home for a while?"

"No, dear. I will be leaving again on Monday morning."

"Where are you going?" Ann asked as she sat down beside her sister.

"I will be going to the mountains to fight the Cherokee Indians."

Margaret took a bite of potato. "Why?"

"The Cherokee have been raiding some settlers, so we have to put a stop to it."

"Oh," Margaret replied, evidently satisfied with his answer.

After supper, the children helped Anna clear the table and wash the dishes while Francis retired to the front sitting room.

When Anna finished in the kitchen and had helped the children change into their nightgowns and nightshirts, they all gathered by the fire.

Matthew, sitting on the floor in front of the hearth, looked inquisitively up at his father. "Father, why do you have to go fight the Indians?"

"Well, Matthew, they are doing some bad things to families that are living in the mountains."

"But why do *you* have to go?"

"Because I am the commander of the militia. I have to lead the men."

"Oh," Matthew replied, satisfied with the answer, as he turned toward the fire to enjoy the warmth.

Addressing all the children, Anna said, "Your father is going to fight the Cherokee so they won't come here. He wants to keep us safe. Now, enough questions. It's time for bed. Go upstairs and get into your beds, and I'll be up shortly to tuck you in."

"Yes, Mother," the children all said in unison as they headed upstairs.

After the children left, Francis turned to his wife and, with a twinkle in his eyes, said. "I'm ready to go to bed, too. Can you tuck me in?"

"I think that can be arranged," Anna replied, smiling as she stood, took her husband's hand, and led him toward the stairs.

As the Rowan County Regiment set out on Monday morning, tensions were high because they expected to encounter Cherokee warriors. Although it was hot and sweaty, the journey was easy for the first two days until they reached the mountains of western North

Carolina. The following two days presented significantly greater challenges, with cooler weather and freezing nighttime temperatures at higher elevations. When they were within a day's march of the first Cherokee town, war cries rang out, and arrows flew.

"Take cover, men!" Francis shouted as he and several officers dove behind some brush beside the trail. One arrow struck a tree next to Francis, narrowly missing him. Shots rang out as the men fired back, repelling the attack. After several minutes, the arrows stopped flying, and the Cherokee war party faded into the woods.

As the men gathered back on the trail, Francis said to his son, Richard, "Major Locke, we are within a mile of the Cherokee town of Coweecho. Take two men and scout the town. Report back to me on warrior strength and the best attack positions. Take precautions not to be detected by Cherokee scouting parties."

"Aye, sir. Matthews and Reynolds, follow me," Major Locke ordered, lowering his body as he crept into the woods.

"At ease, men. Take a rest until they return," Francis ordered as he dismounted from his horse.

At dusk, Major Locke returned and reported to Francis. "Sir, Coweecho is in a valley between two small hills about three-quarters of a mile from here. We spotted approximately twenty men of fighting age, as well as many women and children. There are about ten huts arranged around a central fire pit. The best vantage point for an attack on the town will be from one of the hills overlooking the town."

"Thank you, Richard. Good work," Francis replied as he sat beside the fire, stirring a pot of stew. "You're back just in time. Supper's almost ready."

Before dawn the next day, the militia quietly stalked toward Coweecho, arriving at first light. Cherokee women were stirring, starting campfires, and preparing morning meals. No men were in sight; they were either asleep or away with scouting parties. At Francis's command, the men swooped down on the town by surprise with no resistance. As the militia attacked, Cherokee warriors rushed out of huts, bows drawn, and arrows flying. Women and children screamed and dashed for cover. It was all over in minutes. When the attack ended, several Cherokee leaders were captured, and the huts were set ablaze.

As the regiment moved westward, it encountered several surprise attacks from Cherokee scouting parties. One such assault occurred while the group was crossing a creek. The marauding band charged down from a nearby hill, yelping and shooting arrows at the group.

"Take cover," Francis yelled as he galloped his horse across the creek, dismounted, and ducked behind a large tree, firing his pistol as he ran. "Cover the men in the creek."

The men who had already crossed fired a volley to provide cover for those still in the creek, driving the Cherokee band back with musket fire.

Several wounded Cherokee warriors were taken prisoner, and their injuries were treated before the group continued. As they neared the Cherokee town of Chota, Francis halted his men and dispatched another scouting party to survey the town and devise the best plan of attack.

When the scouting party led by Captain Joseph Dixon returned, they reported to Francis, "Colonel, this Cherokee town is larger than the other one, and they are better protected and fortified. They are in a large valley, so a surprise attack from a nearby hill or mountain will not be possible. Approximately twenty huts in the village are arranged around two council fires in the town center. Also, there are many armed adult men in the town. Still, their bows and arrows will not match our muskets."

Francis was sitting behind his portable desk in the headquarters tent. "Thank you, Captain."

Later that evening, Francis gathered his officers. "Gentlemen, this Cherokee town is larger than the other one and is better protected and fortified. The village has approximately twenty huts arranged around two council fires. Many armed adult men are present in the town. We will divide into two groups and attack from different sides of the village. One group will be positioned on the west side and delay for a few minutes, while the second group will attack from the east to draw the Indians' attention. Then, the group on the west side will attack the rear of the Indians engaged by the group on the east. We should succeed by attacking with both groups from two different sides. We will divide and attack at dawn. Ensure your men are prepared."

The next day at dawn, the men set out in two groups. As planned, one group quietly skirted the town and took a position on the west side, while the other took a position on the east. Francis and several officers concealed themselves behind heavy brush on the south side of the town to observe the attack. As soon as the first group fired a volley into the town, killing several Cherokee men, the town came alive like a disturbed hornet's nest. Women and children ran for cover while the men took shelter and returned fire with arrows and muskets. The attacking group kept firing from behind trees and brush, reloading and shooting again. As expected, the Cherokee focused their attention to the west when the group on the east side of town started firing their muskets. The fighting lasted approximately thirty minutes. When it ended and the smoke cleared, the Cherokee men laid down their weapons and raised their hands in surrender.

"Good work, men. Time to take prisoners and burn the town. Major Dobbs, round up the leaders and burn the huts," Francis ordered as he mounted his horse.

"Aye, sir. What about the women and children?" Major Dobbs asked as he got on his horse.

"Leave them and the warriors, but confiscate their muskets and powder," replied Francis as he rode toward the town.

Several Cherokee leaders were captured, and the huts in town were burned beyond repair. The Cherokee warriors, women, and children were informed about the reasons for their attack and warned against retaliating against white settlers again. Because of this and similar assaults on other Cherokee towns by the Rowan County Regiment and militias from South Carolina and Georgia, the Cherokee retreated further into the mountains, leaving colonial settlers no longer threatened. After nearly three months on this expedition, the Rowan County Regiment returned home for some much-needed rest.

Snow was falling as Francis dismounted, tied his horse to a post, and walked into his home.

Anna jumped up from a chair, ran to him, and kissed him tenderly. "Your home! We've missed you!"

"It is so good to be home. I am tired and cold. It was a difficult expedition, not only because of the cold weather, but my heart is broken for the Cherokee, especially the women and children."

"I am so sorry you had to endure that, but it had to be done. The good news is you're just in time for Christmas!"

"Father, you're home! We have missed you!" Margaret exclaimed as she and the other children ran into the room.

"I have missed you all, too!" Francis said, giving them all big hugs.

"Christmas is next week. We are planning a big celebration with turkey and all the trimmings. Rebecca and Polly will be here with their families," Anna said.

"Richard was with me on the expedition and is now back with his family. I'm sure they will be here too."

"There will be much more to celebrate, with the entire family back together!" Anna replied, holding Francis in her arms.

Christmas that year was a grand celebration with all the Locke family together. There was turkey with all the trimmings, and pumpkin pie. But more importantly, everyone was glad the men were back home safe.

13
Local Loyalists

During a briefing with his officers in early 1778, Francis said, "I have several things to report today. First, as you know, more and more British troops are arriving nearly every month in most American colonies, including North Carolina, and the Loyalists are gaining strength.

"Second, the Continental Army defeated the British Army at Saratoga last October. This was a major setback for the British and a significant win for our cause.

"Third, the Continental Congress passed a resolution declaring that the flag of the United States shall have thirteen stripes, alternating red and white, with a union in the top left corner of thirteen white stars on a blue field.

"And forth, and I'm sure you will be pleased by this, we have been tasked with recruiting and training local volunteers, guarding military supplies, and coordinating with nearby militia groups and Continental Army units to disrupt Loyalist activities and deter enemy recruitment in Rowan County. That means we will stay home for a while!"

After a rousing cheer and much backslapping, Francis continued, "The North Carolina Legislature has passed a law authorizing the arrest of Loyalists and the seizure of their property if they refuse to take a loyalty oath to the Patriot cause."

Francis added, "The good news is that the western part of the county has been separated to form Burke County, so our patrol area is now smaller."

Major Dobbins stroked his chin and quizzically raised his eyebrows. "Colonel, how are we supposed to seize the property of known Tories?"

"If they are unwilling to take an oath supporting our cause, they will be forcibly arrested and removed from their property—whether a farm, a house in town, or a business—and jailed. Then, the property will be turned over to North Carolina. We have the full authority of the legislature," Francis replied.

Major Brandon spoke up. "Colonel, because of the new law, many Loyalists have left the state."

"That is correct, Major. We will identify abandoned properties and turn them over to North Carolina. Also, our ranks are dwindling due to expiring enlistments and furloughs, so we must recruit and train new volunteers to maintain our strength. I have nailed up recruitment posters at several locations in Salisbury. We will train recruits next week. Thank you, gentlemen. You are dismissed."

Francis arrived home at dusk to the scent of wood smoke and supper cooking lingering in the cold air. He dismounted and led his horse into a stall in the barn, removed the bridle and saddle, poured a bucket of feed into a trough for the horse, checked the water tub, and then walked to the house. As Francis entered and walked into the sitting room, Frankie, 11, and Matthew, 7, were on the floor by the fire, playing with toy soldiers.

Frankie jumped up, ran to his father, and hugged him. "Father! You're home!" Francis picked up his son and hugged him. "Yes, I am. Have you been behaving and doing your chores?"

"Yes, sir. I have. Saipo lets me help him feed the horses, and I have been helping Mother gather eggs from the henhouse."

"Good boy," Francis said as he set his son down, removed his hat and coat, and walked out to the kitchen where Anna was peeling potatoes. "I have some good news! We have orders to recruit and train local volunteers, guard military supplies, and disrupt Loyalist activities here in Rowan County. That means I will be home for a while!"

"That is wonderful news!" Anna replied, standing to welcome her husband home with a kiss.

"I thought that would make you happy!"

Anna was glad that her husband would be home for a while. She missed him and worried constantly about his safety while he was away at the skirmishes in South Carolina and then fighting the Cherokee. Francis pulled up a chair by the fireplace and sat down, enjoying the warmth of the fire as Anna continued to prepare supper.

"Francis, I worry about you when you're off fighting, and I worry about our son Richard. How is he doing?" Anna asked.

Francis tended the fire, adding another log. "He's doing well. I imagine he's relieved to be back home with his family for now."

He mentally reviewed the past few months as he sat and watched the new log catch fire. "Richard is an excellent officer who is astute and alert when facing the enemy. I'm proud of him."

Anna tried not to dwell on the dangers this war posed to her husband and son, so she changed the subject. "Saipo and the other men plowed the 200-acre tract along Grant's Creek, getting it ready for planting this spring."

"Good. The next time I go into Salisbury, I'll pick up a few fifty-pound sacks of corn seed," Francis said as he stood and lit candles over the hearth and the kitchen table.

Anna put the potatoes in a pot over the kitchen fire to boil. "Last year, while you were away fighting the Cherokee, Saipo killed and butchered a hog. We've got hams and shoulders in the smokehouse. Would you like some ham with these potatoes for supper? I also have some freshly baked cornbread."

"That would be great! I'm getting hungry," Francis said. "I'll go to the smokehouse and bring in a ham."

"Thank you," Anna said, stirring the pot of potatoes. When Francis returned with a ham, Anna cut off a few slices, fried them, and took platters of ham, potatoes, and fresh bread into the dining room.

"Children, come and eat," Anna said.

As the family ate, the only sounds were the boys' laughter and teasing, accompanied by the crackling of the fire and the wind rustling through the trees outside their home.

Although Anna worried about her husband's safety on the battlefield, she felt a strong sense of pride in his dedication to the Patriot cause, knowing that he was fighting for their family's future and the new United States. Yet, over the past year, when Francis was away, there had been many nights when she tossed and turned in bed, all alone and unable to sleep, wondering if he had been wounded or even killed. News of skirmishes, battles, and rumors of casualties arrived slowly, and Anna felt isolated from the world. The responsibility of managing the household and the farm during his absence made this even more difficult.

She found comfort in daily prayers for her husband and son's safety, for the cause they believed in, and in the support of other women in the area whose husbands were away fighting in the war. She derived special comfort from her two grown and married daughters, Rebecca and Polly, who lived nearby and visited her regularly.

◆◆◆

Early one morning in February, Francis sat on his horse at the edge of a muddy field, observing a line of recruits struggling through musket drills. The recruitment posters had done their job, and the ranks of recruits were filled with farmers, blacksmiths, and young men eager to take up arms against the Crown. With the sun barely above the horizon, frost was still clinging to the ground. The sound of musket fire and smoke filled the air as Francis's officers shouted orders.

"Keep those muskets level, lads!" bellowed Captain James Brandon, his breath showing in the cold air.

Francis pulled his heavy cloak tighter around his shoulders, shook his head, and turned to Major William Davidson, who sat on a horse beside him. "They are green. It will take more than a few days of drilling to make them into soldiers."

Major Davidson gave a knowing nod. "Aye, sir, but they are determined. They will follow you, Colonel."

Francis sighed as his gaze fell on a young boy near the end of the line, struggling to keep his musket steady. "That lad cannot be over sixteen. We'll have to harden them fast. The Tories have been stirring up trouble near Grant's Creek. There are reports of armed Loyalists gathering there."

Major Davidson frowned. "There are rumors that Colonel Bryan's Loyalists plan to raid one of our supply caches in Salisbury. They could cut us off from the Continental Army if they strike there."

Francis signaled to Major James Brandon, the son of his stepbrother, Richard, who was on horseback behind the recruits, and waved him over.

When the major arrived, Francis asked, "James, how many men are ready to march?"

Major Brandon wiped the sweat from his brow despite the chill. "Two companies, sir. If we can keep them fed and armed, another dozen men could join us within a week."

Francis nodded. "We cannot wait. Send word to my brother, Colonel Matthew Locke. See if his men can meet us near Grant's Creek. I want to catch these Tories before they strike."

Major Davidson shifted in his saddle. "And what of the Tory landowners? Based on the new law, we can confiscate the property from known Loyalists."

Francis frowned. He knew he would eventually have to follow the law, even if it meant that the friends and neighbors he had known for years would go to jail. "We'll start with Hugh Graham and Thomas McGuire. They've been supplying Bryan's men with powder and shot. If they refuse to take the oath, seize their property."

Major Brandon nodded. "Aye, sir."

Just then, a scout on horseback galloped up and reined the horse to a halt. "Colonel Locke!" the scout gasped. "A Loyalist band—twenty, maybe thirty men—has been spotted moving toward the Yadkin River crossing. They've got a wagon, probably stolen supplies."

Francis didn't hesitate. "Major Davidson, gather the men. We ride within the hour."

Davidson and Brandon saluted and rode toward the training ground. Francis watched as the young recruits snapped to attention, aware of the shift in mood. He knew that the hard work of rebuilding an army had only just begun, but tonight they would take the fight to the enemy. He guided his horse toward the gathered ranks.

"Men of Rowan!" he shouted. "We have traitors in our land—Tories who steal from their neighbors and serve the Crown. Today, we confront them. Stand together, and we shall be victorious!"

A loud cheer erupted as the new recruits raised their muskets in the air. Francis pulled back on the reins of the horse, startled by the commotion, which snorted, bobbed its head, and stomped its feet.

◆ ◆ ◆

As the militia approached Shallow Ford on the Yadkin River, several men were crossing in a loaded wagon. Francis rode into the water ahead of the rest of the militia and guided his horse in front of the wagon, pistol drawn.

"What are you carrying in the wagon?" he asked.

"Supplies," the driver replied.

"Pull the tarp back so I can see," Francis ordered.

"You have no right to inspect these wagons!" one man yelled.

Pointing his pistol, Francis shouted, "This gives me the right!"

As the rest of the militia arrived and surrounded the wagon with their weapons drawn, the driver pulled back the brake, wrapped the reins around the handle, stood up, and then pulled the tarp off the back of the wagon.

"Those are Rowan County Regiment weapons, ammunition, and supplies from the depot in Salisbury," Francis said as he examined the exposed cargo. "By order of the North Carolina Legislature, you are under arrest for theft and aiding and abetting the enemy. Throw down your weapons. Major Davidson, arrest these men, seize the wagon, and return these supplies to Salisbury."

"Aye, sir," the major replied.

As the Loyalists dropped their weapons, the major, pistol in hand, ordered, "Move to the back of the wagon."

The Loyalists hesitantly climbed onto the back of the wagon and took their seats.

The major turned to Captain Reid. "Captain, take control of the wagon and drive it back to Salisbury."

"Aye, sir," the captain replied as he guided his horse beside the wagon and jumped on.

Taking the wagon's reins and releasing the brake, he turned the wagon around and headed back to Salisbury to return the supplies to the depot. The Loyalists were locked up in the Rowan County jail.

◆◆◆

In April 1778, the dogwood trees were in full bloom when Francis and Major Davidson approached the Graham homestead, closely followed by a dozen men on horseback, muskets loaded and ready.

The modest two-story clapboard house with a front porch sat at the end of a tree-lined dirt road, bordered by plowed fields on both sides and with a hardwood forest behind a barn at the back of the house.

Hugh Graham stood on his front porch; arms crossed over his chest. "Colonel Locke, what business do you have here?"

Francis dismounted and approached the porch. "Hugh, we've been friends for years. We've attended Thyatira Church together. However, I am bound to uphold the law. By order of the North Carolina Legislature, you are to swear an oath of allegiance to the cause of American independence. If you refuse, you will be arrested, and your property will be seized."

"I will not sign an oath, and you have no right to seize my land."

"The law says otherwise. Your son rides with Colonel Bryan's men, and we know you provide them with supplies."

Graham put his hand on the barrel of his musket, which was propped against the wall. "And what if I refuse?"

Francis pulled the pistol out of his belt. "Then you will be arrested, and your property will be seized."

"This is not freedom—it's tyranny," Graham shouted, clearly enraged.

"No," Francis replied. "The British are the tyrants. This is war."

Francis nodded at Major Davidson, who signaled the men to move toward the barn and the main house. Graham's wife and children watched from the window, fear in their eyes. After a long silence, Graham lowered his head and sighed.

"You'll have my land," he muttered bitterly. "But you'll never have my loyalty."

Francis's gaze stayed steady. "Then you're under arrest. Major Davidson, arrest this man and escort him to the Rowan County jail in Salisbury."

As Francis turned and mounted his horse, Davidson rode up, dismounted, and grabbed Graham. "By order of the North Carolina Legislature, you are under arrest for aiding and abetting Tories."

The men of the Rowan County Regiment rode off, leaving the Graham homestead in silence.

Anna was outside hanging clothes on the line when Francis came home that afternoon.

He dismounted and walked over to her. "I just arrested Hugh Graham and confiscated his property at Buffalo Creek."

Anna quickly dropped a wet shirt back into the basket; her eyes widened with surprise. "Oh, no! Why?"

The North Carolina Legislature has passed a law authorizing the arrest of Loyalists and the seizure of their property if they refuse to take a loyalty oath to the Patriot cause. We confronted Hugh at his house this morning for aiding the Loyalist cause, and he refused to stop and take the oath. He has been arrested and is en route to the Rowan County jail; his property will be seized.

Anna was still in shock after hearing the news. "Hugh and his family sat behind us in church just last Sunday! What about his wife and children?"

They will have to move out. Maybe they can stay with relatives. I tell you, Anna; I'm torn between my loyalty to the cause of freedom and the need to arrest some of my friends and neighbors and seize their property when they refuse to take an oath to support the cause. We've known the Grahams for many years, and it saddens me that he and many of our other neighbors continue to support the Crown.

"Francis, you can't punish yourself. You're doing what you believe is right. You must follow both the law and your conscience."

"I know, but that does not make it any easier."

14
The Southern Campaign

On February 10, 1779, during an officers' meeting at militia headquarters in Salisbury, Francis said, "Gentlemen, I've received reports that after their defeat at Saratoga, the British have changed their strategy and are focusing on the South. In December, they captured Savannah, Georgia, and now Augusta. You can be sure they'll move up through Georgia, South Carolina, and then here if they are not stopped."

"It sounds like we'll hit the road again, eh, Colonel?" Major Brandon asked.

Francis looked up from studying the map and glanced at Major Brandon. "Yes, Major. It has been nice being home this past year, but we have been ordered to reinforce the Continental Army and Loyalist units in Georgia to help stop the British advance. According to this map, it'll be a six-day march to Augusta. We might need to help lay siege to that city if our troops haven't already retaken it."

As Francis stood, all the officers followed suit. "We will leave the day after tomorrow at dawn. Please inform your men. That is all."

Francis pulled his horse to a stop in front of his house, dismounted, and walked inside. Anna was sitting by the fireplace, knitting.

"I have some bad news," Francis said as he took off his hat and placed it on a chair by the fire.

Anna set her knitting aside, worry in her eyes. "What's wrong? Is it the boys?"

Francis hated to tell his wife he would be away from home once again. "They are fine. I have just received word that I will be going to Georgia. The militia has been ordered to reinforce the Continental Army and Loyalist units there to stop the British advance."

"Oh, no! Having you at home this past year has been so wonderful! When will you leave, and how long will you be gone?"

"We leave the day after tomorrow. I'm not exactly sure how long I'll be gone, but it will be at least a few weeks."

"Well, I know camp food isn't that great. I'll fix you a nice supper tonight," Anna said.

"That would be nice," Francis said. "It looks like we could use some more firewood on the hearth. I will bring some in from the woodshed after supper."

After eating vegetable beef soup and cornbread, Francis carried several armfuls of wood from the woodshed to the hearth and stacked them while Anna sat by the fire, continuing to knit.

"It gets lonely around here when you're gone," Anna said. "Saipo has been good about keeping the farm running. He keeps the chickens and livestock fed and handles heavy tasks, such as cutting, stacking, and carrying firewood. The girls check on me every week, but it's not the same as having you here."

Francis lit the candles on the hearth and pulled the chair beside his wife, wrapping his arm around her shoulder. "I know you get lonely, Anna, and miss me when I'm gone. I feel the same way when I'm away. Sleeping on the cold ground in tents and enduring the freezing and sometimes snowy weather is tough, and I tire of eating jerky and hard biscuits. Not to mention just being away from you and the children. I miss our talks, your laughter, and holding and kissing you."

I know. Me too. I'm being overly sensitive and hoping this conflict ends soon.

"It will probably get worse before it gets better. The British Army is well-equipped and trained. They are a formidable force, while most of the Continental Army and the various state militias are poorly equipped and undertrained farmers and shopkeepers. And the British are moving north. It won't be long before they enter North Carolina."

Francis and Anna sat quietly by the fireplace a little longer before going to bed. Both knew that the years ahead would be a long, arduous struggle, requiring many sacrifices for the Patriot cause.

The Battle of Brier Creek

The march to Augusta went smoothly, as the men were now used to such journeys. Three days into the trip, the regiment was camped for the night when a rider arrived, dismounted, and entered the headquarters tent.

"Colonel Locke, Private McLeod reporting, sir. I have a message for you," he said as he handed Francis a handwritten note.

Francis broke the wax seal and read the note:

14 February, 1779

Colonel Francis Locke
Rowan County Regiment of the North Carolina Militia

Dear Sir:

Be advised that Loyalists were intercepted and defeated at Kettle Creek, Georgia, on their way to Augusta to support the British. Because of that defeat, the British abandoned the city. We still need your support in Georgia. Please proceed with all haste.

Cordially and forever your servant,
Colonel Andrew Pickens

"Thank you, Private," Francis said. Then, turning to his aide-de-camp, Lieutenant James Campbell, he said, "Lieutenant, please make sure this private is fed and has a place to rest tonight before he returns to his unit."

"Aye, Colonel," the lieutenant replied, leading the private to the officers' mess tent.

Later that night, Francis gathered with his officers around the campfire. "I have received a communication from Colonel Pickens of the South Carolina Militia. A Loyalist force on the way to Augusta has been routed and defeated, resulting in the British abandoning Augusta."

"That's great news, Colonel," Major Brandon replied, warming his hands by the fire. "Does that mean we can go home?"

"I'm afraid not, James. We still need to help monitor the British advance, so we'll keep going bright and early tomorrow."

When the Rowan County Regiment arrived in Augusta, Francis entered General Richard Ashe's headquarters tent and saluted. "Good morning, General. I am Colonel Francis Locke with the Rowan County Regiment of the North Carolina Militia, at your service."

General Ashe returned the salute. "Good morning, Colonel. My men are chasing the British, who have left the city. We hope to catch them near Brier Creek, about 30 miles southeast. We could really use your help if we do."

"Yes, sir. My men are ready. We will move out immediately toward Brier Creek," Francis responded, saluting as he turned to leave the tent.

The Rowan Regiment quickly moved southeast and arrived at Brier Creek by mid-afternoon, where the Americans were repairing the bridge.

Francis approached the officer in charge of the repairs. "Good afternoon, Captain. I'm Colonel Francis Locke with the North Carolina Militia. What happened here?"

The captain saluted, and Francis returned the gesture. "Good afternoon, Colonel. We were in hot pursuit of the British, and they destroyed the bridge after crossing it to delay us. Repairs should be finished by tonight. We'll camp here overnight before continuing the chase."

Thank you, Captain. My men are here to assist with repairs if needed and to pursue the British.

The captain looked relieved. "We could use your help with both."

◆ ◆ ◆

After helping with the bridge repairs, the Rowan County Regiment set up camp for the night. During the night, the British flanked the American position by crossing the creek upstream. As dawn broke, gunfire erupted, catching the American troops off guard. Despite being surprised, the Americans quickly armed themselves and responded to the attack. Francis was standing next to the campfire, sipping coffee when the attack began.

"Take cover, men! We're under attack!" Francis yelled as he threw down his mug, grabbed his musket, and dove behind a nearby tree. "Form a defensive line. Make your shots count!"

He turned to Captain Thomas Lytle, who crouched next to him with his musket resting across his knees. "Captain, how far are the British lines?"

"Less than two hundred yards, sir. They are dug in along the ridge, with artillery pointed straight down the creek. If we try to cross, we'll be cut to pieces."

Francis scanned the treeline, cloaked in fog. Through the haze, he could barely distinguish the red of British coats among the trees and brush. General Ashe's militia had scattered after the first British volley. It was up to Francis and the Rowan County regiment to hold the line or face a complete rout.

Francis looked at Sergeant William Sharpe, a tall man with a scar on his cheek. "Sergeant, how many men are still with us?"

Sharpe knelt beside him, gripping his musket. "Eighty, maybe a hundred. More are scattered in the woods."

Francis rubbed his chin, hesitating briefly, as he was reluctant to make the decision he knew he had to. "We are vastly outnumbered and have no choice. We must retreat or risk losing the entire regiment."

"Colonel!" yelled a young private as he burst through the brush, gasping for breath. His coat was torn, and blood streaked his cheeks. "The British light infantry are moving up the creek, trying to outflank us!"

Francis frowned, thoughts racing through his mind. *If they keep coming, they'll cut off our escape route. We have no choice but to retreat.*

He turned toward Captain Lytle. "We have to retreat now. We have no choice."

Lytle hesitated. "Sir, we can fight and turn them back."

Francis glanced again at the redcoats in the distant fog, the safety of his men foremost on his mind. "No. If we stay here, we will be overrun and killed or captured. Form ranks! Quickly!"
Lytle nodded grimly and stood up. "Company! On your feet! Form ranks!"

The men scrambled out of the underbrush, mud covering their boots as they shouldered their muskets and staggered into rough lines. Francis mounted his horse and led it to the front of the column.

"Sergeant Sharpe, retreat now. Keep your heads down!" Francis ordered.

Musket balls zipped past, slicing through the branches and splashing into the water as the Rowan County Regiment retreated into the swamp, away from the advancing British army. There would be no victory today, but they would survive to fight another day.

By early May 1779, the Rowan County Regiment had returned home after the defeat at the Battle of Brier Creek.

"You're home!" Anna exclaimed excitedly as Francis walked in the front door.

"Yes, but momentarily, I fear."

"How did it go in Georgia?" Anna asked, rising from her chair and kissing her husband.

Francis took off his hat and slumped into a chair by the fireplace, tired from the long ride home. "Not well. The British routed us, forcing us to retreat. My men are discouraged, and I am hungry and worn out from the long trip back. What's for supper?"

Anna stood beside her husband with her hand on his shoulder. "Oh, I'm so sorry, but I'm glad you're safe and home! I didn't know you would be here, so I haven't planned anything. However, I have some pinto beans that I cooked yesterday. I can heat those, and I have some red slaw to go with them."

"That would be wonderful," Francis said as he leaned back, closed his eyes, and quickly fell asleep from exhaustion. Anna went out to the kitchen, stoked the cooking fire, and put the bean pot on it. When the beans were hot, she spooned some onto a plate and topped it with slaw. Then she sliced a piece of bread and placed it on the plate. Walking into the sitting room, where Francis was asleep by the fireplace, she woke him and handed him the plate of beans.

Francis devoured the meal as if he hadn't eaten in days. "Oh, Anna, thank you! This is so good! I have missed your cooking!"

After eating, Francis's energy briefly returned. As Anna sat beside him, he said, "We will probably be called back to help stop the British advance. With the defeat in Georgia, nothing is stopping them from entering South Carolina. I expect to get orders any day."

Anna replied, "You must do what you can to secure our freedom from British tyranny."

She took the empty plate out to the kitchen, washed it, and put it away in the cupboard. When she returned to the house, Francis had fallen asleep again. She didn't have the heart to wake him, so he slept by the fire for the rest of the night.

The Battle of Stono Ferry

In late May 1779, Francis met again with his key officers at militia headquarters in Salisbury. "Gentlemen, the British have now entered South Carolina. Major General Benjamin Lincoln, with the Continental Army, has requested assistance from several militia units to help stop their advance. In particular, we have been called to support defensive operations at Stono Ferry near Charles Town. We will leave tomorrow at dawn. That is all."

The next day at dawn, the Rowan County Regiment began its march to Stono Ferry. Having traveled the road to Charles Town many times while managing his fleet of wagons carrying goods and during past marches, Francis was familiar with the terrain and the route. As a result, the journey was swift and uneventful.

After arriving at the ferry crossing and setting up camp, Francis told Major William Davis, "Major, take several of your men to scout out the British positions to assess their strengths and vulnerabilities."

"Aye, sir."

The major and several men crept through the swamps near the Stono River until they were about 100 yards from the British camp. While lying on the wet ground and hidden behind trees and brush, they assessed the enemy's strength and identified vulnerabilities before cautiously returning to camp.

When they returned, Major Davis reported to Colonel Locke. "Colonel, the British are within a mile of here. We estimate about 900 British and Hessian troops. Indications are that they are preparing for an attack."

Francis quickly gathered his key officers at the headquarters tent. "Gentlemen, the British force is nearby. Position your troops defensively, using the terrain and natural cover to your advantage. We must either stop or, at the very least, delay the British advance and guard critical crossing points."

As expected, the militia faced minor skirmishes with British patrols in front of the army units. These skirmishes hindered the British army's advance, allowing the militia to strengthen their defensive positions.

"Major Dobbs, take your men downstream to flank the British columns and slow their advance," Francis ordered.

"Aye, sir."

As the British approached the ferry crossing, the battle intensified, with cannon and small-arms fire from both sides. The American militia units initially stopped the British advance. However, after about an hour of fierce fighting, Hessian reinforcements arrived and started flanking maneuvers, pushing the American militia back.

Francis and his key officers watched the battle from their horses on a nearby hill.

"We're overwhelmed. The British are now flanking our key positions. Order your units to retreat in an organized manner," Francis ordered.

"Aye, sir," the officers replied in unison as they rode off to their respective units.

The Rowan County Regiment and other local units carried out a well-coordinated retreat, yielding the ferry crossing to the advancing British forces.

Tired and dejected, the Rowan County Regiment headed back to North Carolina. As Francis entered his front door, exhausted and discouraged, Anna greeted him with a hug and a kiss.

"I'm so glad you're back home! I was really worried about you! From the way you look, I guess things didn't go well in South Carolina?" she asked.

Francis removed his coat and hat and hung them up. "The march down there was uneventful. When we reached Stono Ferry, we surveyed the British positions and established our defensive positions. As the British advanced, we held them off for about an hour. The musket and cannon fire from both sides was intense. Then, a Hessian brigade arrived. They started flanking our position, so we had no choice but to retreat. The men are tired and disheartened.

"Nearly 100 of our men were wounded, and at least 25 were killed. Although we slowed the British advance, we didn't stop them. Now, nothing is stopping them from taking Charles Towne and eventually South Carolina. It won't be long before they move into North Carolina."

"I am *so* sorry. And fearful," Anna said. "If the British are not stopped, they will win this war, and you and other Continental Army and militia officers will be hanged as traitors!"

"They *must* be stopped! We can't continue to live under their oppressive rule. We need to keep fighting for freedom."

"Francis, you know I support you and our cause completely, but your safety and having you here mean more to me than independence. I would rather have you here under British rule than be free without you!"

"I would rather be here with you *and* be free! We won't give up the fight!"

For the rest of the year and into early 1780, the Rowan County Regiment enjoyed some well-deserved rest.

15

The Southern Campaign Intensifies

In a meeting with his men in early June 1780, General Rutherford said, "Men, I have bad news: Charles Town fell to the British last month, leading to over 5,000 American troops surrendering. Also, the British commander, Sir Henry Clinton, has been recalled to New York. General Lord Cornwallis has replaced him.

"I cannot stress enough how urgent our cause is. With the British in control of Savannah and now Charles Town, they will be able to supply their troops as they keep marching north through South Carolina and into North Carolina.

"I have also received word that a large group of Loyalists is gathering at Ramsour's Mill, northwest of Charlotte. Colonel Locke, you are to gather men from Rowan, Burke, and Lincoln Counties and disperse the Loyalists at Ramsour's Mill."

"Aye, sir," Francis said as he saluted and turned to carry out the orders.

The Battle of Ramsour's Mill

By mid-June, approximately 1,300 Loyalists, gathered by British Colonel Richard Moore and Major Nicholas Welch, had assembled on the east bank of Clark's Creek near Ramsour's grist mill in Lincoln County, northwest of Charlotte, to organize Loyalists to support the expected British advance into North Carolina. The Loyalists were positioned on a ridge at the top of a mostly open slope. This strategic location provided a clear field of fire for over 200 yards.

Colonel Locke told his scouts, "We are to gather a force and disperse the Loyalists assembled at Ramsour's Mill. Ride to Burke and Lincoln Counties with all haste to request the support of their militia units. We will assemble at Mountain Creek. From there, we will march the 16 miles to Ramsour's Mill."

On June 19, about 400 Patriot militia members, including roughly 100 on horseback from Rowan, Burke, and Lincoln

Counties, moved under the cover of darkness toward the Loyalist encampment at Ramsour's Mill, intent on surprising them.

As they neared the Loyalist camp, Francis and his key officers were on horseback beneath a grove of pine trees. "Gentlemen, we are badly outnumbered three to one. If we attack with the force we have, we will gain the element of surprise. However, if we wait for reinforcements from General Rutherford, we lose that advantage, and we might be defeated. I'm open to any thoughts you may have."

Major Thomas McGuire was the first to speak. "Colonel, with all due respect, we should wait for reinforcements. The Loyalists have an advantage on that ridge. And we will have to cover several hundred yards of open ground to reach them."

Major James Rutherford, one of General Rutherford's sons, replied, "Most of those Loyalists are farmers and shop owners with little battle experience. Our men are battle-hardened. Colonel, as you mentioned, if we wait for reinforcements, we will lose the element of surprise. I say we attack."

Francis took off his hat and scratched his head as he thought for a few moments.

Finally, he replaced his hat, a determined look in his eyes. "We cannot wait. We will attack at dawn. Captain Falls, Captain McDowell, and Captain Brandon, your units will lead the assault on horseback, followed by the other units on foot. Have each man pin a piece of white paper on his hat to avoid being mistaken for the enemy if we engage in hand-to-hand combat. Ensure your men are ready."

The next morning at dawn, thick fog shrouded the landscape as the Patriot militia began their ascent toward the Loyalist positions. As the Patriots moved forward, they met Loyalist scouts posted at the bottom of the slope to prevent a surprise attack. But the Loyalist scouts were caught off guard and fired a quick volley before quickly retreating to their units on top of the ridge. The Patriot militia pushed uphill, catching the Loyalists completely off guard and stopping them from forming lines.

"Press on, men!" shouted Francis as the militia moved forward under mounting musket fire. "We've lost the element of surprise, but this fog will work in our favor."

The mounted units in front quickly moved up the slope on the right to within 30 yards of the ridge, causing panic among the poorly organized Loyalist defensive line. Seeing that the Patriot horsemen were few, the Loyalists regrouped and fired with such intensity that the horsemen had to retreat behind the foot soldiers, who were now halfway up the ridge.

"Keep advancing, men!" Francis shouted through the fog and above the musket fire as the Patriots pressed on with their assault. The Loyalists, driven by the retreat of the Patriot horsemen, launched a chaotic charge down the slope, firing and reloading as they moved forward. Eventually, they met the Patriots on foot, still firing and reloading. The fog and smoke from the heavy musket fire made it hard to tell friend from foe.

The fighting intensified as musket fire gave way to hand-to-hand combat, with men swinging swords, muskets, and axes like clubs. As some Patriot militia members reloaded, their musket fire shifted the battle in their favor, forcing the Loyalist militia to retreat up the hill. During the fight, Francis's horse was shot out from under him, leaving him on foot.

"Keep at it, men! We've got them on the run," he shouted as he fired and reloaded his musket while moving uphill with his men in pursuit of the Loyalists. As the Patriot militia pressed on in the uphill fight, the Loyalist militia eventually broke, leading to a chaotic retreat.

By the time the Patriots reached the ridge's summit, the Loyalists had regrouped behind the ridge and organized a counterattack. The Patriot units on horseback flanked the Loyalists on the right, while the Patriots on foot pressed the attack from the ridge's top. After several volleys of musket fire and intense close combat, the Loyalists were eventually forced to retreat from the battlefield as the Patriot militia units secured the ridge.

After nearly two hours of fighting, the fog lifted, and the smoke cleared, revealing dead and wounded men covering the slope and ridge. About sixty lay dead on the front side of the ridge where the heat of the action occurred. Many more were scattered on the flanks and over the top of the ridge. Both sides suffered heavy casualties, with approximately seventy men killed and about 100 injured on each side. Identifying the deceased was difficult since almost no one was in uniform. Many Loyalists and Patriots were buried where they fell on the hill by grieving family members.

After the battle, the Rowan County regiment returned home to regroup and rest, knowing they would be called to fight again for the cause of freedom.

As Francis rode up the lane to his house, Anna, having heard the galloping of his horse, was standing on the front porch waiting for him.

When Francis dismounted, Anna, overwhelmed with excitement, hurried to him with tears of joy streaming down her face. "I have missed you, and I have been worrying about you! Thank goodness you're home safe!"

The two shared a long, tender embrace before Francis, glad to be home and in Anna's arms again, kissed her affectionately.

"We defeated a band of Loyalists at Ramsour's Mill, but it was very costly. There were many casualties on both sides, and a lot of men were wounded," Francis said as they walked up onto the porch.

"Thank goodness you weren't killed or injured!"

"Several times during the fighting, I could hear bullets whizzing past my head. My horse was shot out from under me, and I had to use my musket as a club. It saddens me that the Loyalists still support the Crown. Many men on both sides have lost their lives in this conflict!"

"I know. It saddens me too, but you must stand firm in your conviction! Even though I worry about you, the dangers you face, and pray for your safety, I still support you in the cause for freedom. We cannot live under the tyranny of British rule!"

As the two of them entered the front door, Anna said, "Why don't you get some rest? I'll go start supper."

"That would be wonderful," Francis replied, taking off his hat and sitting in his favorite rocking chair. "What's for supper?"

"Fried chicken. I've harvested plenty of vegetables from the garden this week, so I think we'll have some corn on the cob, green beans, and sliced tomatoes to go with the chicken. How does that sound?"

"That sounds good," Francis said as he took off his boots. "Where are the children?"

"Margaret and Ann are both upstairs. I think they are reading. Frankie and Matthew are in the barn helping Saipo feed and water the livestock. They will be excited to see you!"

"Don't bother them. I'll see them at suppertime. I'm going to rest a little now," Francis sighed, closing his eyes.

The Battle of Colson's Mill

In early July, General Rutherford reconvened with his key officers at militia headquarters in Salisbury. "There are reports of enemy movement toward Colson's Mill in Stanley County, near the Pee Dee River, a half-day's march from here. We must organize and march there to disrupt the Loyalists' ability to regroup."

Francis spoke up. "General, our force has dwindled to about 200 men."

"You'll have to recruit more men from the local citizens. They will be provided with weapons and ammunition," the general replied.

"Aye, sir."

The next day, Francis established a recruiting office in Salisbury and posted recruitment posters throughout the town. The recruitment effort was successful, and the militia grew to about 600 men by the time they finished training and were ready to head to Colson's Mill.

As the militia approached Colson's Mill in mid-July and the key officers gathered, General Rutherford turned to Francis and said, "Colonel, have a few of your men scout the area for enemy positions, strength, terrain, and natural cover."

"Aye, sir," Francis replied. Then, turning to Major Dobbs, he said, "Major, you have your orders."

"Aye, sir."

When the scouting party returned, Major Dobbs reported, "Sir, the Loyalists have gathered at James Cotton's farm. There seem to be between three and four hundred of them. There is a small, wooded ridge on the west side overlooking the farm, and a mill south of the farm on the Pee Dee River."

"Major Dobbs, divide your men into detachments and position half of them around the mill and the other half in the woods on that ridge to prevent the enemy from retreating in that direction," Francis ordered.

"Aye, sir," Major Dobbs replied, riding off to position his men accordingly.

Advanced scouting parties first encountered the Loyalists, leading to initial skirmishes as the militia assessed the strength of the opposing forces.

General Davidson moved his men north to surround the farm, but they were spotted, and gunfire broke out from both sides. During the skirmish, a Loyalist marksman aimed at Davidson, who was the only man in uniform, and wounded him severely.

"Colonel, General Davidson has been hit!" a scout said as he rode up to Francis, who was watching the battle from his horse in the trees on the ridge.

"Major Harris, take your detachment and flank the enemy on the right," Francis ordered, aware he would need to take charge since General Davidson was out of the fight.

Francis then turned to Richardson. "Major Richardson, move your detachment to the left. I will pull back the central units once you're in position to draw the enemy in. Then, you can surround them from the sides and rear."

"Aye, sir," both majors responded as they urged their horses forward.

With the detachments strategically placed, Francis ordered the central front units to retreat, tricking the enemy into thinking they were fleeing. As the enemy advanced, the flanking detachments moved in, blocking escape routes and securing a Patriot victory.

The battle resulted in three enemy deaths, five injuries, and ten men captured, while the Patriots only suffered two wounded. After the fighting ceased, the Patriot militia took control of the area, helped the injured, and confiscated enemy weapons and supplies.

The Battle of Camden

In the summer of 1780, following the fall of Charles Town in May, British troops under General Cornwallis sought to consolidate their grip on South Carolina. General Horatio Gates, recently appointed commander of the Continental Army's Southern Division, enlisted about 4,000 men—many poorly equipped and inexperienced—and began moving toward Charles Town. Recognizing Gates' approach, Cornwallis moved from Charles Town to Camden, South Carolina, leading around 2,100 British regulars and Loyalists. The British forces were well-trained and better supplied, giving them a clear edge over Gates' troops.

"Colonel Locke, the British are now entrenched in South Carolina and moving north," General Rutherford said during an August meeting in Salisbury with his officers. "Brigadier General Richard Caswell is building defensive works north of Camden, South Carolina, to stop the British advance. General Francis Marion is helping General Sumter with a planned attack on a British supply convoy, so General Caswell needs our immediate support."

"Aye, sir," Francis replied. "I'll muster my men and head to Camden at first light tomorrow."

Later that day, Francis met with his officers at militia headquarters. "Gentlemen, we have been ordered to Camden, South Carolina, to assist Brigadier General Caswell in stopping the British advance. Until now, all the engagements we have been involved in were primarily against Loyalist militia units. In Camden, we will also face hardened British Army units. We will leave tomorrow at dawn."

◆◆◆

When Francis arrived home, Margaret, 18, was reading her Bible, and Ann, 16, was playing a card game.

"Hello, Father!" Ann said.

"Good day, girls," Francis said as he hung up his hat and hugged the girls. "Where are your mother and the boys?"

"I think they are all out in the kitchen," Margaret replied.

Francis walked out to the kitchen, where supper was being cooked. Frankie and Matthew were playing with toy tops on the floor.

"Father, you're home!" Frankie exclaimed as Francis walked in.

"Yes, son. For now, anyway. Have you been good?"

"Yes, Father."

Francis greeted his wife with a hug and a kiss. "Hello, dear. How are you today?"

"I'm fine. How are you?"

"I'm doing well. Unfortunately, I will leave tomorrow morning again at dawn."

"Oh, I'm really sorry. I know it's tough on you when you're away fighting. But I know you must go."

"Yes, I must," Francis said as he sampled some apples stewing in the pot over the fire.

"Where are you headed this time?"

"Camden, South Carolina. This time, it will be different. We will face hardened British Army units. And if we don't stop them, it won't be long before they enter North Carolina."

"Francis, I have gotten used to your being away fighting for the cause, but I still worry about you constantly. I just don't know what I would do if you were to be killed. Please promise me you will take great care while fighting the British!"

"I promise. These stewed apples are delicious! What else is for supper?"

"Fried pork chops and cooked cabbage with the apples. Wash up. Supper's nearly ready. Children, come to the table!"

The next morning, the militia set out at dawn. When the regiment reached General Caswell's camp, Francis entered the headquarters tent. "Good afternoon, General. Colonel Locke with the North Carolina Militia reporting."

"Good afternoon, Colonel. We are building fortifications to stop the British advance. We could use your help," General Caswell said, looking up from a map.

"Also, we need some of your militia to guard our supply depots and key supply routes. Given the scarcity of resources, we must protect food, ammunition, and medical supplies."

"Aye, General. I'll have our men pitch in and help wherever needed."

Addressing his officers, Francis explained, "Gentlemen, you will divide into two groups. One group will help construct defensive fortifications, while the other will guard the supply depots. The fortifications should include earthen embankments, sharpened stakes, and barricades made from felled trees."

The Rowan County Regiment got to work, and by August 16, the fortifications were nearly finished, and the supply depots were secure.

That evening, around the officers' campfire, General Caswell outlined the plan of attack: "Colonel Locke, you will position your troops on the left flank, along with the other North Carolina militia units. Continental Army units will be positioned in the middle, and South Carolina militia regiments will be on the right."

"Aye, sir," Francis replied.

At dawn, the British advanced in their usual formation, firing muskets and cannons, while the Continental Army and militia groups returned fire. However, the British Army was well-trained and disciplined, quickly pushing the militia back to the center of the defensive line. As the British advanced, they launched a bayonet charge. Most of the militia lacked bayonets on their muskets, so, filled with fear, they broke ranks and began a hasty retreat, even though General Gates tried unsuccessfully to rally the fleeing troops. Caught in the chaos, Colonel Locke and the Rowan County

Regiment retreated north alongside other militia groups, abandoning the battlefield. Disheartened and exhausted, they headed home.

Francis returned home, reined his horse in front of his house, and walked inside. Anna greeted him as he hung up his hat and coat. "Welcome home! I've missed you. How did it go in Camden?"

"Not well. The British Army is a formidable force. There was a lot of musket and cannon fire from both sides initially. Then, when the British were within about 50 yards of our position, they charged with fixed bayonets. Since most of our men don't have bayonets, there was nothing we could do but retreat quickly."

"They inflicted heavy casualties on our militia units and the Continental Army. About 900 of our men were killed, and around 1,000 were captured. I believe this was one of our worst defeats."

"I'm *so* sorry. Thank goodness you escaped with your life or serious injury!"

"Yes," Francis replied as he sank into a chair, a frown on his face. "I am so discouraged. Things are not going well for our cause. I felt like we were doing very well after Ramsour's Mill and Colson's Mill, but we only faced militia units in those battles, not disciplined British troops. This was different. Now that the British are in control of Georgia and most of South Carolina, I'm not sure how this war will turn out."

"Francis, you must not lose hope! You're fighting for our freedom! Things will improve!"

"I only hope that as the British move farther away from their supply lines, they will falter. It takes a lot to keep an army on the move in the field."

"Exactly. We can only hope and pray that will be the case!" Anna said. "Now rest up while I fix supper."

The Rowan County Regiment was not called back into service for the rest of 1780, so the men spent some time with their families, and they especially enjoyed a well-earned break at Christmas.

"Good morning!" Anna said, turning to her husband, who was lying beside her in bed. "Merry Christmas!"

"Merry Christmas! I'm really looking forward to the family get-together today," Francis replied sleepily as he turned over, snuggling up to Anna under the covers, holding her close and kissing her tenderly.

Sliding out of bed, Anna said, "I need to get up and start getting ready! The girls, John, and their families will be here before you know it. There's no time for romance this morning!"

"Come back to bed just for a little while," Francis pleaded. "It's cold outside, and the bed is so warm!"

Anna, standing in only her nightgown on the cold floor, smiled, rolled her eyes, and gave a knowing look before slipping back under the covers. "Maybe just for a little while."

Later that morning, Francis brought in firewood and lit the fires in the fireplaces, then went out to the kitchen where Margaret, 18, and Anna were stuffing a turkey.

"Merry Christmas, Father!" Margaret said.

"Merry Christmas! Where are your brothers and sister?"

"They're outside playing hide and seek."

"Can you get a fire going in here so I can start cooking?" Anna asked.

"Sure," Francis replied as he knelt, put some kindling and logs in the fireplace, and lit a fire.

A crisp breeze was blowing the remaining leaves on the old oak tree beside the barn when Francis stepped outside to wish his other children a Merry Christmas.

Ann was standing in front of the barn with her hands over her eyes, counting, "21, 22, 23…". When she finally reached 100, she took her hands away and shouted, "Ready or not, here I come!"

"Merry Christmas, Ann!" Francis greeted.

"Merry Christmas, Father!" Ann exclaimed as she ran around to the back of the barn, searching for her hiding siblings.

Soon, Francis and Anna's older children—Rebecca, John, Polly, and William—arrived with their spouses and children. Including

Margaret, there were eleven adults and about a dozen children at the Christmas celebration.

As the women prepared the Christmas meal, the men and older boys played rounders in the pasture, while the younger ones played outside or sat on the floor playing card games.

"Francis, y'all come in and wash up. The meal is ready!" Anna yelled to the men and boys playing in the pasture.

"We'll be right there!" Francis replied.

While waiting for the men to come in, the women fed the younger children. The meal included turkey with all the trimmings, mashed potatoes and gravy, green beans, corn, and sweet potatoes. Pumpkin pie, of course, was for dessert.

After everyone had eaten their fill, the women washed the dishes while the men and older boys continued their game of rounders, and the younger children played with cards and tops on the floor. As the day ended, it started snowing, prompting everyone to head home.

After everyone had gone and the house was quiet again, Francis turned to Anna. "What a wonderful day this was. It was so good to have the whole family together."

"It certainly was," she replied. "And it was nice having you home from the war."

"I hope this struggle for freedom will end soon, but I'm afraid it will get worse before it gets better."

"I hope not," Anna answered, her voice full of hope.

The Battle of Cowpens

Inspired by their victories at Charles Town and Camden, the British sought to quickly defeat Patriot resistance by rallying Loyalist support in the South. General Nathaniel Greene divided his Continental army, sending Brigadier General Daniel Morgan to the western Carolinas to threaten British outposts, disrupt their supply lines, and hamper British operations in the backcountry. As a result, in January 1781, Lord Cornwallis sent Lieutenant Colonel Banastre Tarleton to pursue and eliminate Morgan's American forces.

Morgan assembled about 1,000 men at Cowpens, South Carolina, near the Broad River, including Continental Army troops and militia from the Carolinas and Georgia, where he planned a strategic ambush of Tarleton's forces.

The night before the battle, after scouts reported Tarlton's forces were approaching, General Morgan visited the campfires of his men and various militia units to give them an update on the war effort, encourage them, and outline the strategy for the upcoming fight.

At each campfire, Morgan would repeat his speech: "Gentlemen, in October, the Loyalist militia commanded by British Major Patrick Ferguson was defeated at King's Mountain, mainly through the efforts of the Overmountain Men. Ferguson was fatally wounded, and his Loyalist militia was destroyed, leading to a decisive victory for our cause."

After much cheering, General Morgan would continue, "Scouts have reported the approach of the British, under the command of General Tarleton. They are a formidable force, but I want to encourage you to be strong and take heart, because we have a surprise in store for them!

"Here is the plan: Militia sharpshooters under the command of Majors McDowell and Cunningham will be positioned on the front line. They are to fire two volleys, mainly targeting British officers, then retreat. Supporting them will be a brigade of the South Carolina militia, led by Andrew Pickens. They are to fire several volleys, then retreat. Both retreats should encourage the British to remain optimistic and continue their assault. When they do, they will face a third line of Regular Continental Army troops commanded by Colonel Howard, with the 3rd Regiment of Continental Light Dragoons, led by Lieutenant Colonel William Washington, in reserve. We shall be victorious tomorrow!"

After General Morgan's inspiring speech around each campfire, the men cheered loudly and went to bed feeling motivated and encouraged.

◆◆◆

The next morning, as the sun peeked over the distant treetops, Francis stepped out of his tent. Looking across the field through the trees, he saw the British Army in their red uniforms forming lines; their bayonets sparkling in the morning sunlight.

"It will not be long now. Make sure your men have their muskets loaded and are ready to go," Francis ordered Majors Barr, Brandon, and Hall, who were gathered around the campfire finishing their coffee.

"Aye, sir. It looks like the British are ready for a fight!" Major Barr said, looking across the field at the red uniforms as he placed a plug of tobacco in his mouth.

"Then a fight they'll have!" Francis replied.

According to Morgan's plan, the sharpshooters positioned themselves at the edge of the field, fully visible to the British forces, while the Rowan County regiment and other militia units took positions behind the sharpshooters. The Continental Army troops then positioned themselves behind the militia, with the cavalry behind them.

With the sun just above the eastern horizon, Tarleton's troops, arranged in their traditional battle lines, launched an aggressive attack, expecting Morgan's force to break and run.

As the British advanced, Major McDowell shouted to his sharpshooters, "Fire at will! Reload, fire again! Retreat!"

As the sharpshooters retreated behind the second militia line, Francis shouted commands: "Hold steady, men! Wait until they are closer."

The British continued to advance: 300 yards, then 200, then 100.

When they were 50 yards away, Francis shouted, "Fire! Reload and fire again. Retreat!"

At that command, the militia fired two volleys and quickly retreated into the woods, reloading as they ran. Some British soldiers fell to the militia's fire; the others kept moving, now faster than before.

Francis mounted his horse and kept shouting orders as the British approached the tree line. The second line of militia fired several rounds and retreated further into the woods. More British soldiers fell, but the rest pressed on even faster.

As the line of redcoats approached the treeline, Continental Army units, hiding behind the retreating militia and concealed by trees and brush, opened fire with their muskets, dropping many British soldiers and causing their ranks to fall into disorder.

Also hidden among the trees, the militia units that had retreated opened fire on the British line. The British, caught entirely by surprise, began a chaotic retreat to the far side of the field. As the smoke from the musket fire cleared, the men of the militia and Continental Army units cheered.

"Excellent work, men," Francis said, riding through his Rowan County Regiment.

When the battle ended, roughly 110 British soldiers were killed, 200 wounded, and over 500 captured. Only 25 Patriots lay dead, with about 125 wounded.

The Battle of Cowan's Ford

In late January, following the American victory at Cowpens, General Greene began retreating north, employing a strategy of avoiding the stronger British army and engaging only when it was to their advantage. The British, led by General Cornwallis, followed the American forces into North Carolina. The Rowan County Regiment, excited about the victory, returned home.

"What an incredible victory!" Francis exclaimed to Anna as he arrived home.

"Wonderful! And even better, you weren't hurt or killed!" she replied.

"We stopped them for sure, but it's not over. It won't be long before they move into North Carolina. I fear for you and the children if the British were to invade Rowan County."

"All the more reason to keep praying and fighting! In the meantime, I'm glad you're home. We have missed you!"

"I'm only home for a little while before I have to go back with the men. What's for supper?"

"I'll rustle up something. Sit by the fire and get warm," Anna answered as she headed out to the kitchen.

On January 30, 1781, a rider arrived at the Rowan County Regiment's camp near Salisbury, dismounted, and ran into the headquarters tent.

"Sir, I have a letter for you from General Greene," the rider said, handing a sealed note to Francis.

Francis quickly broke the wax seal and read the letter, which was addressed: *To the Officers Commanding the Militia in the Salisbury District of North Carolina.*

"Gentlemen," Francis told his key officers, "the British have left Charlotte, and they are moving north. They are about to cross the Catawba River. I have received a letter from General Greene urging us to head to Davidson's headquarters with all haste, and once there, to coordinate with Davidson's efforts to stop the British advance. We will move out in an hour."

When the Rowan County Regiment arrived at Davidson's headquarters, Francis went into the headquarters tent.

"Good afternoon, General. General Greene has ordered me to assist your efforts in stopping the British," Francis said as he saluted.

"Good afternoon, Colonel," answered General Davidson, returning the salute. "Our scouts have reported that Cornwallis is encamped southeast of the Catawba River, waiting for the swollen river to go down. There are several fords nearby along the river, but I'm not sure where Cornwallis might try to cross once it subsides. It will either be Sherrill's Ford, Island Ford, Cowan's Ford, or Beattie's Ford. I think Cowan's Ford is the most probable. I will set militia units at Sherrill's Ford, Island Ford, and Beattie's Ford. Your militia from Rowan will join me, along with units from Mecklenburg County, at Cowan's Ford."

"Excellent, sir," Francis replied.

After an unsuccessful attempt to cross the Catawba at Beattie's Ford because of high water, Cornwallis retreated to a nearby plantation house to wait for the river to recede.

On January 31, despite heavy rains, Cornwallis, eager to continue the pursuit, moved toward Cowan's Ford. He didn't want to waste more time or risk losing the chance to catch the retreating American army. As he approached the river, he saw several fires on the opposite bank in the early morning light, indicating enemy encampments.

There were two potential crossings at Cowan's Ford. Both routes crossed a rocky bottom until they reached the midpoint of the river. Then, the longer, shallower route veered at an angle toward the other side, while the shorter, deeper route went straight across. Impatient to cross and continue their pursuit of Greene, the British kept going straight across the shorter, but deeper, crossing. Because of the still-swollen, raging water, the horses quickly reached their necks, and the foot soldiers struggled in the turbulent current.

Francis had his militia concealed behind trees and rocks on the far bank.

When the British cavalry and infantry were mid-stream and within firing range, Francis shouted, "Fire at will, men."

Several British soldiers fell, but others pressed on across the river. The Patriots kept firing and reloading as they retreated further into the woods. When the British reached the bank, they formed a firing line and launched volleys at the retreating militia. During the skirmish, General Davidson, mounted on his horse, was hit in the heart by a musket ball and died instantly. The battle was brief, and although the Patriot militias could not stop the British advance, they slowed it down, giving General Greene and the American army extra time to retreat northward.

The Skirmish at Terrence's Tavern

In early February 1781, after the British crossed the Catawba River at Cowan's Ford and kept heading north, the Rowan County regiment, led by Colonel Locke, along with other Patriot forces, gathered at Torrence's Tavern, about ten miles east of Beattie's Ford in what is now Iredell County, North Carolina, to regroup and organize resistance against the British troops. As morning rain fell, Francis and several officers sat in the headquarters tent, discussing strategies.

"Colonel, the men complain that their powder is damp from this rain," reported Major Davidson, entering the tent dripping wet.

"There's not much I can do about the rain. Tell the men to keep their powder horns under their coats," Francis replied.

"Aye, sir, the powder in the horns is dry. The powder in their muskets is damp, which could cause misfires."

"Have the men clean the powder out of the muskets. If we are attacked, they can load dry powder."

"Yes, sir. I will make sure they do that," Major Davidson said as he walked out of the tent.

As the men sat around their campfires with unloaded muskets, the sound of horses' hooves in the distance shattered the morning quiet.

"We are under attack! Load your weapons quickly!" yelled Major Barr, leaping up from a campfire and rushing to alert the men.

Before all the men could load their weapons and defend against the attack, the British cavalry detachment led by Lieutenant Colonel Banastre Tarleton charged into the militia camp with swords drawn.

"Fire, then retreat!" Francis yelled, mounting his horse and firing his pistol at the charging cavalry.

The Patriots were caught off guard by this sudden attack, but they held it off temporarily. While some men were still loading powder into their muskets, they were quickly overwhelmed, though most of the men escaped into the thick forest.

The Race to the Dan

General Greene, closely pursued through North Carolina by Cornwallis, was headed toward the Dan River, where he planned to cross into Virginia. Cornwallis was in hot pursuit, trying to cut off Greene's retreat.

The Rowan County Regiment took part in various delaying actions against the British advance and roaming British cavalry units, supporting Greene's overall strategy of attrition. One such encounter took place at Grant's Creek, about four miles west of Salisbury.

"Place the charges on the structural members in the center," Francis ordered, standing beside the bridge over Grant's Creek. As some men placed charges, others ran wires from the charges to a detonator along the creek bank.

Once the charges were set and the wires connected, Francis, moving back to the tree line, ordered, "Blow it!"

The explosion was massive, sending splinters of wood high into the air. Before the smoke had fully cleared, the British dragoon unit, commanded by Lieutenant Colonel Banastre Tarleton, appeared on the far side of the creek, took up positions, and began shooting at the militia.

"Take cover, men!" shouted Francis as he dove behind the nearest tree.

For nearly three hours, the militia held off the dragoons. Eventually, the dragoons crossed downstream and circled to the militia's rear.

Knowing they would soon be trapped, Francis told Major Bayard, "Time to leave! Order your men to retreat!"

The militia quickly retreated west, and the dragoons chased after them for several miles, engaging in skirmishes along the way. Eventually, the dragoons stopped their pursuit and headed north to join Cornwallis and the main body of the British army.

◆◆◆

While Cornwallis was still in Charlotte, the American army, comprising nearly 800 men, wagons, and 500 British or Loyalist prisoners, had crossed the Catawba River north of Charlotte, marched through downtown Salisbury, and crossed the Yadkin River about six miles northeast of Salisbury. After reaching and crossing the Yadkin River at Trading Ford, they gathered and hid all the boats.

After the British crossed the Catawba River at Cowan's Ford, they marched through Salisbury in hot pursuit of the American army. When they reached the Yadkin River at Trading Ford, it was too swollen to cross, and with no boats available, they had to seek another crossing, so they started moving upstream toward Shallow Ford.

"Colonel Locke!" a rider shouted as he approached the Rowan County regiment. "The British are approaching the Yadkin at Shallow Ford!"

"Let's move, men!" Francis shouted as he led his regiment through the dense woods, moving upstream along the riverbank.

As they spotted the British starting their crossing at Shallow Ford, Francis ordered his men into action. "Take cover and fire at will!"

The skirmish was brief. The British returned fire as the Rowan County regiment fired, retreated, and fired again before falling back into the woods, hindering the British army's attempt to cross the river and slowing their pursuit of the American army. However, Cornwallis eventually crossed the Yadkin River and continued his pursuit of the American army.

The Rowan County Regiment and other Patriot militia units continued to follow the British, slowing them down whenever they could. As the militia topped a small hill near Reedy Fork, a tributary of the Haw River close to the Moravian settlement of Wachovia, Francis, on horseback, saw the redcoats trying to cross.

"Men, they are crossing. Spread out and fire at will."

The British formed lines and fired back while the militia took cover and returned fire. As they skirmished, the British advanced while the militia retreated, continuing to fire and reload. Sitting on horseback, out of musket range and next to his key officers, Colonel Locke recognized that the British were gaining ground and closing in on his men.

Concerned for their safety, he ordered his men to retreat. "That's all, men. We've done our job in delaying their reaching the American army. Time to go."

In mid-February, General Greene's army crossed the Dan River into Virginia at Boyd's Ford. The Rowan County Regiment had considerably delayed the British, who arrived a day late at the Dan River on February 15.

In early March 1781, General Greene's army faced the British, led by Brigadier General Isaac Huger, at Guilford Courthouse near present-day Greensboro, North Carolina. Although costly, the battle ended in a British victory.

While the Rowan County regiment played a key role in disrupting British operations earlier that year, their service ended before the Battle of Guilford Courthouse, so they were not involved in this critical fight. By April, the Rowan County Regiment of the North Carolina Militia had returned home to their families.

16
Life in the New Nation

In early April 1781, Francis and Anna's oldest daughter, Rebecca, visited Anna. Anna was sitting by the fire in the sitting room, knitting.

"Good morning, Mother. How are you today?" Rebecca asked as she walked in.

Anna laid down her knitting. "Good morning. I'm alright. How are you?"

"I'm fine. Have you seen the latest copy of the North Carolina Gazette?"

"No. Is there an article I should be interested in?"

"There is an article about a big battle at Guilford Courthouse last month. The British won that battle, and over 1,000 patriots were killed. That was several weeks ago!"

"Oh, no!" Anna moaned, tears welling in her eyes as she set her knitting aside. "Your father isn't home yet. I've been hoping and praying he isn't injured or killed. I hope he wasn't involved in that battle!"

"I'm sure he's fine. You must not worry until you know for sure."

"I can't help it!"

A week later, as Anna sat rocking in a chair on the front porch, worried and watching for her husband, she saw a horse and rider approaching on the road. Francis rode up to the house, pulled his horse to a stop, and dismounted. He paused there for a moment, reflecting on the past several years with pride and satisfaction: the battles he had fought, the many times bullets had whizzed past him, narrowly missing, the lonely days and nights away from his wife and family, the lives of the men he had trained and fought alongside, and what their sacrifices had meant for freedom.

Anna, overwhelmed with happiness to see him, jumped up and ran to him as he approached the front porch steps. "You're home! I'm so thankful! I've missed you so much!"

Throwing down his pack and removing his hat, Francis embraced his wife and kissed her tenderly. "I have missed you and the children, too!"

"I was so worried about you! The North Carolina Gazette had an article about a major battle at Guilford Courthouse, stating that there were many casualties." Anna whined, with tears of happiness in her eyes.

"Yes, there was a battle, and many men were killed, but my regiment was not involved," he replied. "Enlistment terms expired, so the regiment disbanded before that battle."

"So, you will be home now, for good?" Anna asked hopefully.

"Yes, dear. I'm home for good!"

"What about the war? Do you have to continue fighting?"

"Cornwallis is not in a position to continue pursuing Greene as he did throughout North Carolina. Reports suggest that the British have gone to Wilmington to resupply and recuperate, and they will probably head north into Virginia from there."

"Oh, that is wonderful!" Anna replied with a wide grin as they walked inside, arm in arm.

"Are you hungry?" she asked. "There's some fried chicken and a few biscuits left over from yesterday."

"Yes, that would be great!" Francis replied as he settled into the rocking chair by the fire. "I *am* a little hungry. And exhausted!"

Francis's two youngest, Frankie, now 15, and Matthew, 11, were sitting at a table playing cat's cradle with some string.

"Father, did you shoot anyone?" Frankie asked.

I'm sorry to admit that I did, Francis. War is a horrible reality. Men on both sides are killed or wounded fighting for what they believe in. I never wanted to shoot anyone, but I fought to ensure we could live in a free country.

◆◆◆

In early November 1781, a rider approached as Francis was cutting and splitting firewood near his barn. "Colonel Locke! Colonel Locke!" he shouted, pulling his horse to a sudden stop before leaping off.

Francis drove his axe into the chopping block and turned to see what the commotion was about.

"Colonel Locke, great news! American and French forces defeated Cornwallis at Yorktown, and he surrendered. The war is over. We have won!" the rider shouted, rushing toward Francis.

Francis paused for a moment, reflecting on all the times he was away from Anna, the many nights sleeping on the cold ground, fighting Loyalists and British troops with bullets whizzing past his head, and the men under his command who had been killed. He whispered a quiet prayer, thanking God for bringing him home safely to his loving wife.

"Great news! Thank you!"

As the rider mounted his horse and quickly rode away, Francis ran to the house to share the good news with Anna and the children.

Not finding her in the house, he ran back out to the kitchen. "The war is over! Cornwallis surrendered at Yorktown!" Francis cried as he opened the kitchen door and rushed inside.

Anna was lifting a pot off the kitchen fire. "That's wonderful news!" she shouted as she set the pot on the hearth.

Running to him, she threw her arms around him and kissed him tenderly.

Francis lifted Anna off her feet and twirled her around. "No more fighting! No more British oppression!"

"I am so happy the war is over! It will be nice having you home for the holidays, and home for good!" Anna exclaimed as she gave her husband another long kiss.

◆◆◆

In April 1783, Francis stopped by the law offices of William Polk in Salisbury to discuss his will.

"Good morning, William. How are you today?" Francis asked as he stepped into the office and removed his hat.

"Good morning, Francis. I am well. The first draft of your will is ready for your review."

"Great," Francis replied. "I figure it's time. I'm getting old, and I don't know how many years I have left. Some days, when I return from working in the fields, I'm completely worn out. Farming is tough work. I'm getting too old to work that hard every day."

"Francis, with your background as a sheriff, county coroner, and militia officer, you might consider studying law and becoming a lawyer. Sitting behind a desk isn't as physically demanding as farming, and it's much more profitable," William replied.

"Hmm... I might consider that. But how do I start?"

William reached into his bookcase, pulled out a few books, and handed them to Francis. "Here are some basic law books. You can start by studying them."

"Thank you," Francis said as he took the books.

William continued, "After you have studied these books, if you're still interested, I will take you on as an apprentice. I could use some clerical help here in the office, and that will give you a chance to learn the business."

"That is very gracious of you!" Francis replied. "Thank you!"

"You might also consider taking a night class in Latin, which will help you understand some legal terminology."

"Excellent suggestion. I believe the Zion-Parnassus School, which is part of Thyatira Church, offers that class."

After William reviewed and revised the draft of the will with Francis, Francis thanked him, put on his hat, and stepped outside, now looking at his life and future with a new perspective.

Returning home, Francis hung up his hat and sat down beside Anna, who was sitting by the fireplace mending a sock.

"I had an interesting meeting with William Polk," he began.

"Oh? Has he finished your will?"

"He had the first draft ready for review. We made a few changes. He will prepare the final copy for my review."

"Good. So, why was *that* so interesting?" Anna asked, now curious.

"Well, he suggested that at my age, I might want to give up working in the fields day after day because it is so physically demanding."

"Then what would you do?"

"William suggested I might want to become a lawyer, which would not be as physically demanding. He gave me some law books to study and offered to take me on as an apprentice! He also recommended that I take a class in Latin."

"That is a very kind offer! I worry about you when you get up every day before dawn, work all day in the fields, and come home at dusk completely worn out. I think you should take William up on that offer!"

"Thank you. I believe I will."

The following week, Francis's brother, Matthew, a Brigadier General in the North Carolina militia, dismounted his horse in front of Francis's house and walked inside. Francis was sitting at the dining room table, drinking coffee.

"Good morning, Francis."

"Good morning. How are you and your family?" Francis replied, "Would you like some coffee?"

"Yes, please."

Francis poured coffee into a mug and handed it to Matthew. "What brings you here this morning?"

Matthew took the mug of coffee and sat down at the table. "Thank you. I wanted to let you know I will be attending the North Carolina General Assembly session in Hillsborough next week. I will return when business concludes in May. Can you check on Mary and the boys from time to time?"

Francis sat down and took a sip of coffee from his mug. "I would be glad to."

Matthew set his mug on the table. "How are you occupying your time these days, now that the militia has disbanded?"

"I spend a lot of time in the fields with Frankie and Saipo, plowing and planting. When not in the fields, we are in the barn fixing equipment or caring for the cows, horses, pigs, and chickens."

The two brothers sat drinking coffee and talking about the weather, farming, and local politics.

Francis poured Matthew another mug of coffee. "At night, I've been doing some reading."

"Reading? Reading what?"

"I was at William Polk's law office in Salisbury last week. I told him I was getting too old to work in the fields every day. He suggested that, given my background, I might want to consider studying law and becoming a lawyer. He also offered to take me on as an apprentice. I'll start next fall after the harvest."

"That is great!"

"I will also take a night class in Latin."

"Wonderful!" Matthew exclaimed as he finished his coffee. "I wish you well!"

Then, standing, he said, "I must be going. I need to prepare for the trip to Hillsborough. Thank you for the coffee."

"You're welcome. Have a safe trip. Don't worry about Mary and the boys. I'll check in with them from time to time," Francis replied as he stood and walked Matthew to the door.

In February 1784, Francis was sitting at his desk in William Polk's offices in Salisbury, reading the latest issue of the North Carolina Gazette.

As William entered the room, Francis said, "This article says that the Congress of the United States has ratified the Treaty of Paris."

"That's good news. That means the war is officially over, and they will disband the Continental Army," William commented, sitting down and looking at Francis. "Will you resign your commission as colonel of the militia?"

"Yes. There's no need to keep it, since I won't be taking up arms anymore. I did my part to secure our freedom. Besides, I'm getting too old! I'll send a resignation letter later this month."

As William Polk's apprentice in the 1780s, Francis gained expertise in criminal and civil law, torts, contracts, drafting briefs and motions, and court procedures. He also improved his communication and interpersonal skills to interact effectively with clients, opposing counsel, and the courts.

One morning in April 1789, Francis's brother Matthew, who had been in Philadelphia as a member of the Continental Congress, walked into the law offices in Salisbury.

Francis was sitting behind his desk, studying a contract. "Good morning, Matthew."

"Good morning," Matthew replied, taking a seat.

"So, how did it go in Philadelphia?"

"It went well. The session of the Continental Congress ended last week. The last state, Rhode Island, ratified the new Constitution proposed by the Constitutional Convention. We are now officially the United States."

"That is great news, Matthew!" Francis replied. "It has been a long struggle for freedom."

"Yes, it has, but we still have a lot of work to do."

Francis leaned back in his chair. "That is true. I hear a new town is being planned in Wake County to be the new state capital of North Carolina."

Matthew crossed his legs. "Yes. The State of North Carolina has purchased 1,000 acres from Joel Lane for the new town. They will call it Raleigh, named after Sir Walter Raleigh. They are laying out the streets, which will be named after towns and counties in North Carolina. One street will be Salisbury Street. Another will be Rowan Street. A new state capital building will be in the center of town, where the State House and Senate will convene. Construction is expected to begin later this year."

"It will be nice to have the state capital a little closer than some of the other places, like Halifax, Hillsborough, or Fayetteville," Francis observed.

"Yes, but I still have to travel to Fayetteville this year to attend the Senate," Matthew reminded.

Then, changing the subject, Matthew asked, "How do you like being a lawyer?"

"I'm enjoying it. Most of my work involves assisting folks with estate planning, land purchases, and other legal matters. Sometimes, I go to court to defend clients in criminal or civil cases."

"I wish you well. How is Anna doing?"

"She is well. Just getting old like the rest of us," Francis answered with a smile.

"And the children? Are they all well?"

"They are all doing well. Frankie and Matthew are the only ones still at home. They are almost grown. They help Saipo manage the farm for me. How is Mary?"

"Mary is doing well, but she doesn't like my being away from home so much."

"Anna didn't like my being gone either during the war."

Matthew stood up. "Well, I guess I should get going. I've got to be in Fayetteville for the opening session of the Senate next week, and I have a lot to do before I leave. I'll drop by to see you when I return."

Francis stood and walked his brother to the door. "Thank you for stopping by and updating me on current events. Good luck as a North Carolina senator."

"Thank you. It was good catching up with you, Francis. Take care," Matthew said as he tilted his hat and headed out the door.

In late May 1791, as Francis and Anna were finishing breakfast, Matthew reined his horse in front of their house and walked inside.

"Good morning!" Matthew said as he took off his hat and sat down at the dining room table.

"Good morning. I didn't expect to see you. Is the House of Representatives not in session?" Francis asked, finishing a bite of bacon.

Anna's housemaid, Rose, came in with a fresh pot of coffee. "Good morning, Mr. Matthew. Would you like some breakfast or some coffee?"

"I've already eaten, but yes, coffee would be nice. Thank you, Rose."

As Rose poured Matthew a cup of coffee, he turned to Francis and announced, "The House of Representatives is in recess. I have returned home because President Washington is on his southern tour, and he is scheduled to pass through Salisbury in a few days."

"Yes, I heard that yesterday at the courthouse. Are you planning on greeting him when he arrives?" Francis asked, sipping his coffee.

"As a member of the United States House of Representatives from North Carolina, I'm part of the welcoming committee. I stopped by to see if you'd like to join me. President Washington is trying to meet and thank as many men as possible who fought for our freedom."

"Meeting the President of the United States would be a great honor," Anna said as she took a bite of bacon.

"Yes, it would," Francis replied. Then, turning to his brother, "I would love to, Matthew. Do you know the exact date he will be in Salisbury?"

Matthew sipped his coffee. "He is expected in Salisbury on the 30th. That's the day after tomorrow. He will stay overnight at Hughes' Hotel, and a reception and dinner are scheduled there at 7:00 pm."

"I will be in court in Salisbury that day. I can meet you there."

"Alright. I will see you there at 6:45 pm," Matthew said, finishing his coffee and standing to leave.

On May 30, Francis finished his business at the courthouse and walked across Main Street to Hughes' Hotel, a two-story stone building with large stone steps leading up to the entrance. Francis removed his hat as he opened the heavy oak door and stepped into the lobby.

Matthew was standing beside the stairs leading to the upstairs rooms. "Good evening, Francis. Glad you could make it. Many dignitaries are already in the dining room, where the president will be received. There is Charles Bruce, the Intendant of Police here in Salisbury; Spruce May, whom you know because he is also a lawyer; Richard Steele, a United States Congressman; James Brandon, Lieutenant William Brandon's son, and many more."

"This is exciting. Let's go in."

As the group gathered in the hotel dining room, President Washington, his secretary Tobias Lear, and several attendants entered to applause.

President Washington exemplified the qualities of a distinguished leader and statesman. His shirt was made of fine white linen with full sleeves. There was a ruffled lace neckcloth tied at his throat. His tailored, cream-colored waistcoat was adorned with matching cloth-covered buttons. Over the waistcoat, he wore a dark blue wool coat with brass buttons. His tan pants ended just below the knee, and he wore silk stockings that reached his feet, covered by polished black leather shoes with silver buckles. A fine gold pocket watch, attached to a gold chain, was in a waistcoat pocket, and his powdered hair was tied back in a ponytail with a black ribbon.

The reception committee had formed a receiving line, and as the President and his entourage walked along it, being introduced and shaking hands, he finally reached Matthew and Francis.

"Good evening, Mr. President. My name is Matthew Locke. I am a retired brigadier general in the North Carolina militia and a member of the United States House of Representatives. It's an honor to meet you, sir," said Matthew, bowing.

"It is a pleasure to meet you, General Locke. Thank you for your service in the fight for our freedom," President Washington replied, "and thank you for serving in Congress."

Turning to Francis, Matthew continued, "Allow me to introduce my brother, Francis Locke. Francis was a colonel in the Rowan County Regiment of the North Carolina Militia and is now a lawyer here in Salisbury."

"Good evening, Colonel Locke. Thank you for your service in the militia. Hmm... I remember hearing about a Colonel Locke involved in a fight against local Loyalists at Ramsour's Mill. Was that you?"

"Yes, sir."

"That was a decisive victory for us. If I recall correctly, it completely demoralized the Loyalists here in North Carolina, causing many to abandon the fight, and encouraged local Patriots to keep fighting! Well done, Colonel!"

"Thank you, sir."

"I also recognize the efforts of your Rowan County Regiment in slowing Cornwallis's advance through North Carolina as he chased after General Greene. Your actions played a vital role in delaying the British, giving General Greene time to regroup in Virginia."

"It was all for the cause of freedom, sir."

After President Washington greeted everyone, they all took their seats, where a lavish meal of roast beef, potatoes, carrots, onions, and freshly baked rolls was served, complemented by a delightful French Cabernet Sauvignon. Following the meal, President Washington addressed the group, sharing his vision for the future of the new United States and expressing gratitude for the warm welcome and hospitality.

After the president retired to his room, Francis and Matthew said their goodbyes and headed home, feeling uplifted and hopeful about the future of the new nation.

In 1794, after ten years working as a private attorney in William Polk's law offices, Francis finished arguing a criminal case before Judge Samuel Spencer and was walking toward the courthouse door to return to his office.

Judge Spencer stopped Francis in the hallway. "Francis, do you have a moment?"

"Yes, sir. Is there a problem?"

"No. I want to discuss an opportunity with you if you have time."

"I always have time for you, sir," Francis replied.

After the two walked back to Judge Spencer's chambers, the judge removed his robe and sat behind his desk, signaling for Francis to take a seat.

The judge cleared some papers off his desk, then said, "William Sharpe has resigned as State Attorney for Rowan County. If you're interested, I would like to appoint you to that position."

Francis looked at the judge, hardly believing what he was hearing, and wondered, *Did I understand the judge correctly? If so, am I even qualified for such an honor?*

"Yes, sir, if you believe I am qualified, I would be honored to be considered," Francis replied.

"You are indeed qualified. Over the years, I've been impressed by how you argue cases in my courtroom, your understanding of the law, and your dedication to justice. I'm confident that you will fulfill the responsibilities of that office exceptionally well. As the highest-ranking judge on the Rowan County Supreme Court, I appoint you State Attorney for Rowan County."

"Thank you, sir. I accept," Francis answered.

"Good. I will complete the paperwork. William Sharpe will vacate his office by the end of next week. You may assume that role and move into his office the following Monday. You can keep the existing staff, or you may choose to hire your own," Judge Spencer said.

Then, standing, the judge added, "I am due in court to hear another case. That is all."

"Thank you, sir."

After leaving the courthouse, Francis strolled down the street to his law office, lost in thought and filled with a deep sense of pride and satisfaction. *Could this really be happening? I came to America as a young boy, faced hardships to start a new life in the backcountry of North Carolina, married and raised a family, built a home with my own hands, farmed the land, successfully started and managed several businesses, served as sheriff and coroner, held the rank of colonel in the war for independence, and became a successful lawyer. And now, this honor?*

When Francis entered his office and took a seat, William Polk was sitting behind his desk, reviewing a legal document. "William, I have some bad news and some good news."

William looked up with a concerned expression on his face.

Francis continued, "The bad news is I will tender my resignation effective the end of next week."

"Oh, no! Why?" William exclaimed as he dropped the legal document on his desk.

"Because of the good news. I have been appointed State Attorney for Rowan County."

William, grinning broadly, stood, approached Francis's desk, and extended his hand. "Congratulations! I hate to lose you, but that is great news. You're an excellent lawyer and will do well in that position."

Returning home that evening, Francis shared the good news with Anna.

"Oh, that's wonderful, Francis! You've worked hard all your life and truly deserve this. I'm confident you will serve with honor. I am *so* proud of you!"

Francis spent several successful years as the State Attorney for Rowan County, representing the people of Rowan County in criminal and civil cases.

In June 1796, Anna suddenly became ill with a mild fever, stomach cramps, and severe diarrhea.

"Francis, I'm sick, and I feel terrible! I have diarrhea and excruciating stomach cramps. Go fetch Dr. Bartlett in Salisbury," Anna said as she lay in bed, moaning.

Francis, concerned about his wife's condition, quickly saddled his horse and rode into Salisbury to fetch the doctor. The doctor was right behind in his buggy as Francis returned and dismounted. With his medical bag in hand, the doctor followed Francis upstairs and into the bedroom, where Anna lay, clearly in pain.

After examining Anna and noticing her symptoms, the doctor said, "She's got the bloody flux."

Then, after mixing a vial of laudanum and giving it to her, the doctor said, "Make sure she drinks plenty of water, and keep her as comfortable as possible. There is really nothing I can do except bleed her, but in my experience, that will not help her condition. I will return tomorrow to check on her."

"Thank you, doctor," Francis said as he escorted the doctor out the door.

After the doctor left, Francis drew a bucket of water from the well and carried it up to the bedroom where Anna lay, still moaning.

"Drink this," Francis said, offering Anna a cup of water.

"I can't. I'm hurting so much from these cramps."

"You must," Francis replied. "The doctor said you should drink plenty of water."

"If I must," Anna replied, taking the cup and drinking the water.

Worried about his wife's well-being, Francis watched over Anna, caring for her day and night, yet she continued to decline.

"Francis, I feel like I'm getting weaker every day, even with your care," she said feebly.

On June 24th, the doctor returned and was greeted at the door by Rose, Anna's housemaid.

"I'm here to see how Anna is doing," the doctor said as he entered the house.

"Sir, Mr. and Mrs. Locke are both upstairs. I can show you to them," Rose replied.

Walking upstairs to the bedroom, the doctor found Francis in bed beside Anna, moaning and clearly in pain.

"Doctor, thank you for coming. I think I've caught the same thing Anna has. I feel terrible, and I also have terrible diarrhea."

Recognizing that Francis was quite ill with the same symptoms as his wife, the doctor told Rose, "Send for Anna's daughter, Rebecca, and have her come at once."

Seeing that Anna was pale and unresponsive, the doctor checked her pulse and breathing. Finding none and realizing that she had passed away, he looked at Francis and, with deep sorrow, said, "Francis, I am so sorry to have to tell you this. Anna is deceased."

Francis, with tears streaming down his face, slowly turned over, hugged his late wife, and gently kissed her forehead. "Oh, Anna! I love you so much! I'm so sorry!"

When Rebecca arrived in her riding chair, she rushed to the bedroom, only to be stopped by the doctor at the door.

The doctor's voice trembled as he said, "Rebecca, I wish I didn't have to tell you this, but your mother has passed, and I am afraid your father has the same ailment."

"Why?" Margaret asked, sobbing with tears streaming down her face. "What happened?"

"It is the bloody flux. I suspect their well water may be contaminated. There was nothing I could do."

Crying uncontrollably, Rebecca ran into the room, leaned over, and gently hugged her mother, tears dripping onto the pillow. Francis, lying there, moaning and incoherent, suddenly realized Rebecca was in the room.

"Rebecca, your mother has passed away. I'm so sorry!" he said. "And I'm in a lot of pain in my stomach and have diarrhea."

"I know, Father. She's gone. She was such a sweet lady. I will miss her, and I know you will too. But I'm now worried about you!"

After Anna's body was removed, Rebecca stayed to comfort and care for her father. However, after several days, his condition had worsened. On June 27, three days after Anna died at age 61, 74-year-old Francis Locke passed away with Rebecca by his side.

◆◆◆

The usually clear, bright summer sky was gray and cloudy, and a chill hung in the air as mourners made their way into the double funeral service at Thyatira Presbyterian Church. As the organist played 'Amazing Grace' and the congregation stood, Francis and Anna's brothers, sisters, children, and grandchildren slowly walked down the aisle to their seats up front. Rebecca wore a black dress and a simple hat; her tear-streaked eyes were hidden beneath a lace veil. An American flag with 15 stars and 15 stripes draped Francis's casket. Anna's casket, decorated with lilies, sat next to his. The church was filled with the sweet scent of the many flower sprays that adorned the altar.

The minister approached the pulpit after the family and congregation had taken their seats. Opening his Bible, he quoted Jesus from John 11:14: *Do not let your hearts be troubled. Ye believe in God; believe also in me. In my Father's house are many mansions. If it were not so, I would have told you. I go to prepare a place for you.*

Then, closing the Bible, he said, "Let us pray. Lord, we come today to celebrate the lives of Francis and Anna Locke. They were both pillars of the community and good and faithful servants. Francis was an honorable man and a loving husband and father. Anna was a devoted wife and mother. They were both taken from us too soon. May God rest their souls. Amen.

"We gather today not only in grief but also in gratitude," the minister said, looking into family members' teary eyes, "to commemorate the life of Colonel Francis Locke, and to celebrate the life of Anna, his faithful wife of 47 years.

"Francis was a generous man who served his community, state, country, and family, and was a model citizen in Rowan County. As a young man, Francis led his mother and siblings along the Great Wagon Road, arriving here with almost nothing. He bought land and started a farm, building a house and barn with his own hands. He was a businessman who, along with his brother Matthew, founded a transportation company that brought English-made goods into our community. Later, he operated a tavern where community members could gather and relax from their daily stresses. He served as sheriff and coroner for our county.

"Let us not forget the sacrifices he made for freedom. Called to serve our young nation, Colonel Francis Locke bravely and honorably led the Rowan County Regiment, contributing to the defeat of the British and Loyalists in the Carolinas, and was the hero of the battle at Ramsour's Mill.

"After the war, Francis became a lawyer, providing legal services to the residents of Salisbury and Rowan County. Because of his legal knowledge and expertise, he was appointed State Attorney for Rowan County. In that role, he represented the people of Rowan County in many civil and criminal cases.

"Above all, Francis Locke was a caring son and brother, a devoted husband to his wife Anna, and a loving father and grandfather, passing down a legacy of love, honor, and service to his family.

"Anna was a devoted wife and loving mother. Let us not forget the sacrifices she made in the pursuit of freedom. During her husband's wartime absence, she diligently maintained their home, took charge of the farm, raised their young children, loved and supported her adult children and grandchildren, and prayed faithfully for her husband's well-being and for our young nation. When Francis was home from the fighting, she cared for him, comforted him, encouraged him, and reassured him that the fight for freedom was honorable and just. Francis was the love of her life, and she showed this in everything she did for him."

After this inspiring eulogy, the minister finished with a prayer and concluded by saying, "Lord, we commend their spirits into Your loving arms. Amen."

The organist played 'Abide With Me' as the family filed out, followed by the congregation.

An unseasonably cool rain was falling as the family and mourners slowly made their way to the cemetery behind the church.

When everyone was gathered beside the graves, the minister said, "Let us pray," and offered a prayer of hope and salvation as the caskets were lowered into the ground.

Veterans of the Rowan County Regiment folded the flag that had draped Francis's coffin. When the flag was presented to Rebecca by General Griffith Rutherford, Francis's former commander, she broke down and sobbed uncontrollably.

About the Author

Eliott Secrest is a historian, genealogist, and storyteller with deep roots in North Carolina—the same soil that once bore the footsteps of Revolutionary patriots. In his debut book, *Patriot Colonel: The Life & Times of Francis Locke*, Eliott highlights one of America's overlooked heroes, blending meticulous research with a compelling, rich narrative. A lifelong student of history, Eliott has spent years uncovering forgotten stories and bringing to life historical figures, locations, and significant events from North Carolina's past. With a talent for bringing the past into sharp focus, he revives the stories of those who shaped his home state and a young nation, making sure their legacies live on.

Acknowledgments

First, I'd like to thank my wife, Melody, for the countless hours she dedicated to reading, reviewing, and sharing her insights from a woman's perspective. Her input truly enriched the characters and added depth to the story's emotional impact. I also want to thank my granddaughter, Ashley, who offered valuable feedback and suggestions that enhanced readability.

Although the dialogues and personal interactions in this work are entirely fictional, the life of Francis Locke, the norms and customs of the 18th century, and the skirmishes and battles of the American Revolution are based on historical records. To ensure accuracy, I consulted many sources, including historical works, state archives, and a wide range of websites too numerous to mention. For those interested in learning more about the history of this period, I recommend:

Rouse, Jr., Parke (1995), *The Great Wagon Road, From Philadelphia to the South*, The Dietz Press, Richmond, VA.

Blethen, H. Tyler and Wood, Jr., Curtis W. (n.d.), *From Ulster to Carolina, The Migration of Scotch-Irish to Southwestern North Carolina*, North Carolina Department of Cultural Resources, Office of Archives and History.

Ramsey, Robert W. (1964), *Carolina Cradle Settlement of the Northwest Carolina Frontier, 1747-1762*, The University of North Carolina Press, Chapel Hill, NC.

Thorpe, Daniel B. (1996), *Taverns and Tavern Culture on the Southern Colonial Frontier: Rowan County, North Carolina, 1753-1776*, The Journal of Southern History, Volume LXII, No. 4.

Buchanan, Richard (1997), *The Road to Guilford Courthouse: The American Revolution in the Carolinas*, Richard Wiley & Sons, Inc., New York, NY.

A Revolutionary War Southern Campaign map is available at www.alamy.com. Image ID: D6AGTK.

For more information, to book an event, or to join my mailing list, contact me at:
    Email: eliottsecrest@gmail.com
    Website: https://www.eliottsecrest.com/
    Facebook: www.facebook.com/eliottsecrest